Swimming in a Sea of Stars

Other Books by Julie Wright

Regency Romance

A Captain for Caroline Gray

Windsong Manor

Contemporary Romance

Lies Jane Austen Told Me

Lies, Love, and Breakfast at Tiffany's

Glass Slippers, Ever After, and Me

Swimming in a Sea of Stars

JULIE WRIGHT

SHADOW
MOUNTAIN
PUBLISHING

Visit us at shadowmountain.com

Library of Congress Cataloging-in-Publication Data
(CIP data on file)
ISBN 978-1-63993-101-9

Printed in the United States of America
Lake Book Manufacturing, Melrose Park, IL

10   9   8   7   6   5   4   3   2   1

To all those who struggle to feel their own worth,
value, and place in this world.

You have worth.
You have value.
You have a place.

To quote Linkin Park:
"Who cares if one more light goes out
in a sky of a million stars?"

The answer is that I do. I care.

Please do not deprive the world of
the good that you bring to it.

Stay and shine!

Addison's Journal
December 6, 4:14 p.m.

Dear Diary,

Oy, I just penned the stupidest opening to anything in the world. I cannot believe I just wrote that. "Dear diary . . ." As if I'm a thirteen-year-old girl smacking pink bubble gum under a too-bright sun glaring off a bedazzled journal cover. I'm seventeen. I hate pink. I would rather die than have a bedazzled anything.

Wow.

What would my therapist say about that sentence? *I would rather die . . .*

I have to go to school tomorrow. I have to face everyone. And the only thing my therapist is arming me with is this diary. She says if I document all the times when I feel stressed or insecure or afraid or sad, I'll be able to understand those feelings better, and I will be able to work through them. The therapist said I'm special and this diary will help me figure it out. But how can a diary and a pen I stole from the therapist's office make me special? I think we could actually finish this exercise with that little tidbit right there. A diary is not special. Petty theft is downright embarrassing.

It is a nice pen, though. I'm keeping it.

The therapist asked me to call her Alison. I don't. I don't know what that says about me. I don't think writing any of this is helping, but I'm not really in a position to argue. She's "The Therapist," and I'm just "The Girl Who Tried to Kill Herself." That's what they will all say when I get to school—"There goes the Girl Who Tried to Kill Herself." I don't think there is anyone left in the state of Massachusetts who hasn't heard about the Girl Who Tried to Kill Herself.

They'll speculate as to why. And they'll all be wrong.

They'll say it was a bad home life.

Not true.

They'll say it was bullying and talk about all the mean girls and boys who walk the halls of public school.

Not true.

They'll say it was a boy who didn't return my affections.

Not true.

Maybe true.

Sort of true.

I don't know what's true.

I remember this poem I read in English class once. It was by a British lady named Stevie Smith about someone in the middle of the ocean trying to catch the attention of the people on the shore. But the man who was in the ocean hadn't been waving. He'd been drowning. I think about that poem a lot because I am in the ocean, waving frantically. But no one's waving back at me. I'm out here alone.

Maybe that's not true either. I have my mom.

But she's so busy being busy. She works a lot to keep us both fed, to keep a roof over our heads. It's not that I don't appreciate her. I am so grateful for all she does and who she is. Which is why I wonder . . . how much better would her life be if I wasn't here anymore?

That's the question I want to ask my therapist, but I'm afraid to. Because though I think I know the answer, I don't want to hear it. I don't want to hear that my mother would be better off without me.

The reason she cries at night? That's all me. She won't find herself someone to love in the way married people love each other. She won't find someone because she is protecting me. Which means she's alone. She's in her own ocean drowning, and that's my fault.

Drowning. School is tomorrow, but I'm drowning.

Nobody heard her . . . the dead girl.

But I'm not dead. I'm still drowning.

· ·

Booker Williams

Matt opened the front door and entered the house without knocking or ringing the bell. Not that Booker cared. Matt was there all the time. Booker's mom and dad joked about sending Matt's parents a bill for all the food Matt ate.

"Did you hear the news?" Matt swept his ashy blond hair away from his pale face and grinned as his backpack hit the hardwood with a thunk that would have made Booker's mom cringe if she'd been home. She wasn't home. She'd left to take his little brother, Nathan, to hockey practice.

"What news?" Booker barely paid attention because the sooner he emptied and reloaded the dishwasher, the sooner he and Matt could hit the family room and kill zombies for the rest of the day. If he didn't get chores done, his mom would be killing him instead of him killing zombies.

"About Addison."

Booker dropped the glass he'd been about to set in the cupboard. He caught it before it hit the counter and stared at how the brown of his skin reflected through the faceted glass. His hand trembled.

How had his best friend turned into a gossip queen when it came to anything to do with Addison Thoreau?

"Is she okay?" He hated how his heart rate jumped to a sprint at the sound of her name. He wanted to grab his friend by his shoulders and shake the answer out of him. He also wanted to order Matt out of the house because the last time Matt had asked him if he'd heard what had happened to Addison, Matt had told him how Addison had been rushed to Nashoba hospital because she had tried to kill herself.

"Yeah. She's fine. I guess. As fine as someone who tried to land themselves a permanent residence in a cemetery can be."

Booker blinked several times into the cupboard before he could look at Matt. "So, what's the news?"

"She's coming back to school tomorrow."

"Seriously? How do you know?"

"Chloe."

"How does Chloe know? She's not friends with Addison. Do they even know each other?"

Matt kicked off his shoes, each one thunking to the ground next to his backpack. "The bigger question is, how come you didn't know? Dude, you work in the office too. Why is it I learn everything from Chloe? Especially this! Addison and you were, like, a thing. You should have been the first to know. I swear, man, it's like you don't even work at Silver River. What's the deal?"

Booker couldn't argue. Chloe had access to all kinds of information that Booker never seemed to hear so much as a whisper about. They might have worked as office aides together, but Chloe was clearly better at sleuthing than he was.

And for him to know nothing about Addison returning to

school? How could he have missed *any* information regarding Addison?

"We weren't a thing," Booker said. It was his automatic response anytime anybody mentioned it. After Addison's attempt, it was the only thing anyone wanted to talk to him about.

"Right. Sorry. I forgot you were still in denial."

Before Booker could thump Matt upside the head for being stupid, Matt had already moved on to more interesting topics, specifically Chloe and if she would be willing to go out with him.

"She's out of your league, man," Booker said with a smirk.

"How do you figure?"

"She dates nice guys."

"I'm a nice guy."

Booker grinned at his friend. "Not when there's witnesses. You can't be a jerk and assume people know you're using 'jerk' as your cover story so that no one knows you're hiding the nice guy underneath."

Matt made a *psh* noise and pulled the orange juice carton from the fridge.

Booker stopped him before he was able to drink from it. "Dude! Get a glass."

"I was gonna waterfall it."

Rather than explain how his mom wouldn't be any happier about that, Booker grabbed a glass and handed it to Matt.

He didn't mention Addison again. He wanted to. He wanted to talk about her until his voice box bled, but he couldn't say anything about her without feeling guilty or stupid or weird or all three.

Besides, what could he say? *Do you think Addison's attempt was my fault?* No. Sometimes not talking about the things in his head meant he didn't have to deal with the things in his head. And it couldn't have been his fault. He'd done everything right. His mom and dad had taught him how to respect girls.

He tried to put aside the news of Addison's return to school and just hang with his friend. His mom came home an hour later and poked her head around the corner of the family room. Her black braids were tied up in a red wrap, and her gold jewelry jangled at her wrist as she waved at them.

"Thanks for doing your chores, honey. Matt, always good to see you."

"Thanks, Momma Williams. And the leftover pie was awesome."

She laughed. "If you feed them, they will come."

Still smiling, she headed for her office. Soon, Christmas carols came from down the hall, along with her rich voice crooning along to "Silent Night." His mom loved her Christmas music no matter the time of year. At least it was December, which made her listening seasonally appropriate. It was cringey when she played holiday tunes loud in June.

Booker's little brother, Nathan, tried to inject himself into the zombie-killing fest but got called out again by their mom because he had his own chores to do. That was the way in Booker's family. They played as hard as anyone, but chores came first.

Booker's family lived a comfortable life, but because his parents believed in hard work, they made sure their children did too. And they named their boys after men they felt were good examples of ethics and education. Nathan was named after Nathan Francis Mossell, a Black doctor who worked to train more Black nurses and doctors, and who championed the cause of his people. And Booker was named after Booker T. Washington—an educator who advised presidents. It was a lot to live up to, but Booker was trying. He might not have aspirations to be an educator who advised presidents, but he had every intention of being a veterinarian. It was why he volunteered at the animal shelter several times a week.

Matt didn't bring up Addison again until he was stuffing his feet into his shoes to head home. "So how do you feel about her coming back? Will it be weird for you? You know, after everything she did to you?"

The question startled Booker. Everything she did to him? What had she done to him? Booker was pretty sure people at school gave him the stink eye because they thought *he'd* dumped *her*—that she was the jilted girlfriend or whatever. But the truth was, neither of them had done anything to the other.

At least he didn't think so.

"Nothing. She didn't do anything to me, man."

"So . . . You're really not weirded out or anything?" Matt's face scrunched in disbelief.

"Should I be?"

Matt shrugged.

"Tomorrow's probably going to be a hard day for her. I plan on making it as easy as possible. I'm hoping you're planning to do the same."

Matt shrugged again. "I'm not going to school tomorrow. Wisdom teeth. But I'll follow your lead when I get back. I'm on whatever side you're on. Brothers." He held out his fist.

"Brothers." Booker tapped his dark-brown knuckles to Matt's pale ones, and they both snapped their fingers at the contact. It was their personal handshake, subtle and cool. Booker always smiled when he saw other people mimicking the knuckle-bump-snap.

Matt left, and Booker felt his smile sag into a frown. "Whatever side I'm on," he whispered. What side *was* he on?

He wanted to say he was on her side. But he'd found it harder and harder to be on her side after her attempt, especially when his cousin Sebastian had been diagnosed with Hodgkin's lymphoma. Life and death felt immensely more personal than ever before.

His phone buzzed with an incoming text. He glanced at it, expecting it to be Matt with the declaration that he'd forgotten something and needed Booker to bring it to school.

It wasn't Matt.

It was Seb. *"Sup cuddy bro? You gonna be there tomorrow?"*

"Wouldn't miss it," he texted back.

"You really gonna shave your hair off with me?"

Booker looked in the mirror in the front hall. He liked his hair. The black coils that hung just past his ears were a source of pride, but he loved his cousin more.

When Seb had been diagnosed with Hodgkin's lymphoma, Booker hadn't really known what everyone was saying or why everyone looked so stupid depressed. When they called it by the name Booker understood—*cancer*—he was wrecked, but he couldn't show it. Seb needed him.

Later, when he was alone, he'd uncharacteristically punched a wall and broken his middle and ring fingers on his right hand. He flexed those fingers before responding to his cousin. They didn't hurt much anymore, but they still popped.

"Absolutely," he texted back. *"Gotta settle the question once and for all."*

"What question??"

"Which of us has a more attractive-shaped head. I mean, we know it's me, but I'm willing to humor u."

"Since I'm the dying one, right?"

Booker ground his teeth together and blinked away the burn behind his eyelids. *"Man, don't think u can change the subject by trying to get me to feel all sorry for u. Just admit it. My head is more attractive."*

"No pity. No mercy either. Just wait until u see my fine, bald head tomorrow night. U gonna be so jealous."

"As jealous as u of my man coils."

"I could have coils if I wanted."

Booker laughed. Seb preferred the look of a short fade. Had he ever let his grow out? *"Right. Man, you're halfway to bald anyway."*

"Which is how we know bald looks good on me. I've always figured u were hiding some freaky shape under that Rapunzel mane of yours."

"We'll see." He walked up the stairs to his bathroom and was brushing his teeth when another text came in.

"Thanks for being there for me, Book."

Booker considered the text from his cousin, who also happened to be one of his closest friends, and couldn't help but compare the two hard things he had to face tomorrow. Addison coming back to school after her attempt, and Seb shaving his head so that his hair loss was his choice and not something chemo chose for him. One trying to shrug out of the life she was given versus the other clinging desperately to keep his life.

"I'm totally weirded out," he said out loud, finally confessing the truth to his bathroom mirror. Because like it or not, tomorrow was coming, and Addison would be there, standing in the middle of that tomorrow. He didn't know if she liked him and wanted to see him or if she hated him and wanted him to disappear into the deepest well. He also didn't know if he liked her and wanted to see her or if he really resented her for making him feel like her attempt was his fault.

He sort of wished he was at the bottom of the deepest well because then he wouldn't have to face the girl he wasn't sure he understood anymore.

Would he hug her and tell her he missed her? Or would his heart be indifferent?

Would she hug him and tell him she missed him? Or would she treat him like the enemy?

Only tomorrow knew.

Addison's Journal
December 7, 7:26 a.m.

Dear Diary,

Right now, Mom is downstairs making me breakfast. She needs to be at work in thirty-four minutes. Well, thirty-two now. She wants to drive me to school so that I won't be alone. I appreciate it. I really do. But I'll still be alone because she will drop me off and go to work, where she will likely get in trouble for being late. And I will have to enter that building by myself.

Well, maybe not exactly by myself. After all, I have this diary and the pen I stole from my therapist's office. For the first time in my life, I'm wondering about that whole pen-mightier-than-the-sword thing. Can a pen save me from myself? Will it save me from everybody's curious looks?

I have become a curiosity, like the bearded lady or the tree man from circuses of old.

Everyone will stare. Everyone will wonder.

My old friends don't know how to talk to me. Some of them stopped talking shortly after visiting me in the hospital. I think they were afraid suicide might be contagious. It's been long enough now that no one talks to me except my mom. Well, and my therapist. But she doesn't count because she's being paid to talk to me. Seriously, isn't the fact that I have a therapist enough of a reason to know I'm not ready for this?

But then, I'm never going to be ready even though going back was totally my idea.

I told them I was ready. It's been a month. Mom's used all her time off from work. I have to be ready.

Maybe no one will notice me. I'm wearing a long-sleeved hoodie over a long-sleeved shirt. Both go all the way to my fingers so the scars aren't visible. Maybe no one will see.

But isn't that part of the problem?

The therapist asked me if I felt like I was alone. I didn't answer. How *can* I answer that?

Yes, I feel alone. But it's so much more than those four words.

She also asked me if I kept secrets. I'd made a joke of that, telling her that my mom was paying her to keep my secrets, not for me to keep hers. She'd been patient with the joke. She'd even smiled. She has nice teeth. She was obviously better about wearing her retainer than I have been about wearing mine.

Mom is calling. Breakfast is ready. It's time to do this. Whatever people do or do not see or notice . . . It's time.

As far as secrets . . . I definitely have them. Who doesn't?

• •

Celia Martin

Celia startled awake. Nothing new there. Though she never remembered her nightmares, she knew her sleep was as plagued by stress, anxiety, and demons as her daylight hours were. What she didn't know was whether her daylight demons were also awake. Was she safe to get out of bed? The answer to that determined whether she could go to school.

She stayed still and listened intently for any sound.

The refrigerator moaned—death throes that seemed to go on and on forever. Someday, those rattling threats would give out altogether, and Celia would wake up or come home to the smell of rot.

Fact: She had come home to that smell a lot, and it had nothing to do with the fridge dying, just her mother forgetting she'd left food on the counter.

Celia carefully lifted her head from her too-flat, stained pillow to listen harder.

She held her breath until she heard the sound she was looking for: her mother's soft snore from the living room couch.

Today was a school day after all. At least it was if she hurried and if she stayed quiet. She hated leaving the warmth of her covers to face the icebox air of her house, but she'd hate staying home even more.

She felt around the floor until her fingers found a shirt. She hurried to yank off her mother's hand-me-down Led Zeppelin T-shirt she always slept in and tugged the mostly clean shirt from the floor over her head. She didn't have to worry about any of her other clothes. She slept in her bra, jeans, and tennis shoes. She would have slept in her own shirts too, except that would make them smelly and more wrinkled than normal.

Moving through her house in the dark as often as she did left her feet vulnerable to the debris of jagged bottle caps and the sharp edges of crumpled beer cans. Even crushed potato chips could cut a bare foot if stepped on the wrong way. Besides, sleeping in shoes meant she was ready to run if she had to.

Celia was lucky in many ways. She knew that. She'd never had to run before. None of her mom's boyfriends had exactly been kind over the years, but even the worst ones had only laughed while her mom belittled her and sometimes hurt her. None of them had ever moved to join in.

Not until this new one anyway. This new boyfriend had a mean streak. Her mother's anger had escalated from the typical verbal slashings and mental torture to yanking hair and occasional slaps across the face. It had settled now into indifference. Was it weird that indifference hurt more than anything else?

Fact: It was very weird.

She took a shaky breath. The burns were healing. That was the important thing—the thing she had to focus on. Soon, the red wounds would be white skin again, even if it was scarred.

She pulled her hair into a ponytail without bothering to comb it, wrapped her fingers around her frayed backpack strap, and silently slipped to the back door. Before she was able to get the door closed, she heard the rustling of her mother moving on the couch.

Her heart plummeted to her stomach. Her extremities went numb as she fumbled with the door, finally getting it closed, and then tripped down the icy front steps in her haste to get away. The weight of tense terror that the door would open behind her, that her mother's iron voice would yank her back inside, nearly pinned her in place.

She didn't breathe until she'd made it down the street and around the corner. Her mom never had enough energy or ambition to actually chase Celia down and drag her home again. If she made it out of eyeshot, she was free. And by the time she returned from school, her mom would have forgotten her fury over Celia going in the first place.

Usually.

Not always.

Fact: Those days were bad days no matter what Celia did or didn't do. It had been a week since her mom's last really bad day.

As that thought came to mind, Celia noticed the breeze flowing through her shirt. She never wore a jacket because she didn't have one—even in the winter. She was used to the cold. However, the way this cold pushed its way to her skin and took bites out of her was different. She looked down and gasped, a cloud of vapor puffing out in front of her face.

No.

No, no, no, no!

Tears sprang to her eyes as she put her finger to one of the several cigarette holes in the white pullover shirt. How had she accidentally grabbed *this* shirt? How had she not felt the rough edges of each hole when she'd pulled it on?

Celia drew in a deep breath and squeezed her eyes shut against the memory of her mom's new boyfriend sucking on a cigarette. He'd grabbed her and pressed the smoldering tip through the shirt and into Celia's arm.

Celia had cried out, and her mom's eyes had met hers. But then her mom had looked away again. She hadn't done anything to stop her boyfriend even though he did it several more times.

It had been the first time her mom had allowed anything to really hurt Celia, to hurt her bad enough to leave marks that didn't yellow and fade within a few days. The shirt had been one of Celia's favorites before. The blank canvas of the white had seemed full of possibilities. Now it was a pocked, marred surface—an ugly reminder of a moment she wanted to forget.

Celia had thrown the shirt away that night, but her mother had found it and tossed it back in her room, yelling about how there was no reason to throw away good clothes. Her mom ranted for more than an hour about how hard she worked to keep clothes on Celia's back.

Fact: All of Celia's clothes were thrift-store finds or hand-me-downs.

Fact: Her dad's monthly child-support check never went to support anything for her.

She'd left the shirt where her mother had thrown it on the floor.

Celia glanced back toward her house but didn't falter in her steps. Her mother had been waking up, moving around. If Celia was there when her mother actually got off the couch, there would be no school for her that day.

"I can do this," she said out loud. She poked a finger through one of the other holes. Maybe it looked like the destruction had been deliberately designed. People wore pre-holed pants. Why couldn't they wear pre-holed shirts?

She growled at her mother under her breath, but really, this was her own fault. The shirt had been on the floor for more than a week in the closet-sized room she called her own. She should have picked it up.

The burns on her skin were healing, sort of. A couple of them were worse than the others because when the cigarette had been sucked on before being pressed against her skin, it burned hotter somehow. Those weren't healing well at all.

Which made being at school so much better than being at home. When she was in class, her wounds had more time to heal. Every day she made it out the door and safely inside the school building, she felt as though she won a battle.

Fact: There had been more than 230 skirmishes and battles leading to America's independence. So what if her own independence required so many more skirmishes, so many more battles. More than two hundred thousand men fought in the Revolutionary War. She fought her war alone. Maybe if someone was fighting alongside her, her war would move along faster too.

You don't have to fight alone.

The thought came unbidden to her mind. She physically shook her head to make it go away. She couldn't tell. She *wouldn't* tell. What good would telling do anyway?

Fact: She'd end up living with her dad and his new wife, and wouldn't that be worse?

Maybe.

She felt almost sure it would be. His new wife didn't like Celia. Celia was sure of it. At least her mother pretended to care. And some days, her mom seemed as though she actually liked Celia.

She shook her head again, and as she rounded the corner of Silver River high school, she ran into someone. Literally. She ping-ponged off the person and into the brick wall before she caught her balance. She felt a hand grab her arm, helping to keep her on her feet.

"Whoa. You okay?"

She looked up and saw Damion Archer. A popular kid, not just by high school standards but by first-world standards. He was internet famous, creating sarcastic political and social commentary cartoons on his YouTube channel. It didn't hurt that he was also the stereotypical hot guy every girl in high school fell for: dark hair, dark eyebrows, dramatically pale skin, inquisitive brown eyes that made him look mischievous and interesting. She didn't know why he even still went to school. Chances were good he made more money than his parents.

She shook her head again so she could focus on him. He'd asked her a question.

"I'm fine," she said, keeping one hand against the cold, rough, red brick while hitching her backpack strap over her shoulder. The strap, which had been hanging on by its last thread for nearly a year, snapped at that exact moment. Gravity sucked the pack to the ground. She heard the small mirror she kept in the side pocket shatter, and she closed her eyes as if somehow everything in the day would reset while she wasn't looking.

She opened her eyes, expecting to see Damion looking at her backpack, maybe trying to figure out how to fix whatever had obviously broken, but he wasn't looking at the ground. He was looking at her—at the sleeve of her shirt.

"Shirts make a lousy filter," he said.

She looked down, her face feeling sun-surface hot. Now that he'd drawn attention to it, she could see the smudges and stains from its time spent in the garbage as well as the burn marks from where the cigarette had eaten through the cloth and into Celia's skin.

"I don't know what you're talking about," she said, trying to sound as frosty as the air between them.

"Your shirt. Looks like you tried using it as a smoking filter."

"I don't smoke," she said, injecting more ice into her tone than before.

"Right. I get it. You don't smoke, but your shirt does." Then he laughed as if he'd made an amazing joke.

Why did people follow this idiot on YouTube? They couldn't actually think he was funny, could they?

He frowned when he realized his audience of one hadn't clapped for him. "Hey, seriously, you okay? You don't look like you're okay. I can get you some help." He glanced around, his gaze stopping when he saw the school officer. He waved his hand to catch Officer Whitfield's attention.

Celia's insides swirled into a mass of panic. "No!" she shouted and snatched up her broken backpack. "I don't need your help."

She fled, the sounds of Damion and the officer calling after her ringing in her ears.

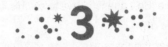

3

Addison's Journal
December 7, 8:11 a.m.

Dear Diary,

How long does it take before something becomes an addiction? I'm three entries into this journaling thing, and I'm already writing again.

We're in the car, and Mom is sooooo late for work. She's told me a dozen times that she'll be available if I need anything, that she can be to the school in minutes if there's trouble. I want to tell her to just turn around and take me home.

Oh, her supervisor just called, and now Mom is driving and talking on the phone. I can't tell her to turn around when she's already late.

So instead, I'm rehashing all the splintered fragments in my head.

Maybe I don't want to rehash anything.

The worst part about having a therapist? They want you to rehash. They ask all the prying questions—the ones that don't have answers, or at least don't have good-enough answers.

I might throw up. Is it too late to transfer schools? I should have waited until after the Christmas break to go back. Why did I convince my mom and the therapist that I was ready?

People would be less likely to notice me after the Christmas break because everyone will be coming back at the same time. But Mom doesn't have any more time off available. And she's afraid to leave me home alone. So I guess I have to do this.

What am I afraid of?

I can almost hear the therapist asking me that question: "What are you afraid of, Addison?"

Everything.

I am afraid everyone will notice my return.

I am afraid no one will notice.

I am afraid I'll be assigned to someone so they can babysit me.

I am afraid of . . .

Everything.

. . . .

Damion Archer

Damion stared after the girl who'd bumped into him, freaked out, and then ditched. He shrugged at Officer Whitfield, whose ear warmers were skewed on his head so that only one ear was entirely covered.

"I guess she's good," he told the officer.

Officer Whitfield gave him a thumbs-up and then smiled broadly at him, his nose and cheeks red in the frigid air. "You're hitting it out of the park with Inside-Out Archer. Your last episode on the nightmares of winter survival camp was genius! My wife and I laughed for the rest of the night after watching it."

Damion smiled. "Thanks, man. I appreciate you watching." He was still surprised by how well his comedy animations had taken off.

Officer Whitfield smiled and raised his thumbs-up a little higher, as if he was afraid Damion had somehow missed it, so

Damion gave him a thumbs-up back and went on his way. The winter survival camp episode *had* been pretty awesome. He was proud of how it turned out.

He checked his watch and groaned. Between the morning catastrophe at home and the weird literal run-in with the broken-backpack girl, he'd barely have time to make a quick Instagram post linking people to his new Inside-Out Archer video on his YouTube and TikTok channels before he had to get to class. He didn't want to end up in detention—*again*. The amount of time he spent in the derelict building was more than enough. No reason to add minutes he didn't have to spare.

He made his way to his locker and checked the mirror he had tucked inside before finger combing his hair and pulling it into that messy look girls seemed to like. He stood with his back to the overcrowded hall at school and posed with his signature half grin that people had come to expect from him. He snapped a selfie against the backdrop of students desperate to get where they were going. He slid his fingers over the screen to caption his new post. "Winter Survival Camp: High School Style. Because we're all trying to survive something this winter." He then plugged his new video and made the post. He sighed over how pale he looked on camera and vowed to spend some time in the sun.

Before he could even close up his locker, a chime sounded and a slight buzz shook his phone. Damion smiled. He loved that messages for his posts came so instantly. He felt relieved with each comment, with every like, with every forward, though he would never admit it out loud. Those little digital approvals filled him up in a way nothing else did. Some people had other coping mechanisms for their troubles. He had his fan base.

He read the message. "Damion! OMG You look AMAZING today!!!! ♥ Marry me!"

"Hey, Archer, got a second?" Avery Winters raised an eyebrow from where she'd been leaning on a nearby locker, apparently watching him. She shoved off it and moved closer.

He put his phone down, scowling at the girl who'd been the equivalent of a dislike button being clicked repeatedly in his real life. It still startled him to have to look down to see her face. He'd grown a lot over the last two years, while she remained a little shorty. He would've called her a *cute* little shorty, but since she hated him and he wasn't entirely sure the feeling wasn't mutual, she didn't deserve the compliment. Small consolation: she seemed paler than he did. He wasn't the only one spending too much time indoors.

"Do you need something?" A little of the satisfaction that came from the noise of his phone as it collected approval from his fan base ebbed at having to deal with Avery.

"It's what I have that you need."

He stepped back, nearly knocking over someone who'd been crossing behind him to get to their locker, and scowled. "I think you're confused, *Frosty Winters*. I have standards, and you don't make the cut."

"Ew. And seriously? That old nickname? Don't be such a child."

"I was a better child than some people who think it's okay to steal other people's go-karts."

"You need to stop poking that bruise. It's time to heal, Archer." She shook her head, making her black hair flip over her shoulders. She'd dyed it last summer. If he was being honest, he liked it—not more than her natural brown hair, but at least as much.

23

"Why are we having a conversation?" he asked. "Don't you have drugs to sell to kindergartners or something?" It was a low blow considering her brother had been arrested for fentanyl possession a few weeks ago, but it was out, and he couldn't call it back. He hated that sarcasm was his first response. Not that there was anything except sarcasm between the two of them. Not anymore.

She narrowed her eyes but shrugged. "I was actually trying to do you a favor, but if you don't want it, fine. Whatever." She started to walk away.

"Wait!" he called before she could disappear into the crowd. He glanced at his phone to check the time. He was going to be late to class, but Avery hadn't talked to him in forever. Maybe longer. A lot of time had passed between when they had been kids and best friends to now when she was a day away from juvenile detention and he was on his way to a solid career as a comedy animator.

"What favor?" he asked.

"I know you're on the Hope Squad."

"Everyone knows that." Sure, he never wore the school-issued purple sweatshirt because no one could make that scratchy mess look good, but people knew the details of his extracurriculars. It was his job to make sure people knew everything about him so they would feel like they were his friends so they would remember his name.

His phone chimed again and again. He ignored it and focused on the girl in front of him.

"That girl who tried to kill herself awhile back? She's coming back to school today. If you actually care about what it means to be on the Hope Squad, you'll talk to her, help her out."

"You friends with her or something?"

Avery narrowed her eyes at him as she tightened her grip on her books—a pre-algebra math book and an English book.

It was weird enough that she had physical copies of her books instead of digital, but why was she taking pre-algebra in high school? Didn't the school system make all students get that out of the way back in seventh grade? As he wondered if she'd had to take it again for some reason, she sort of answered his original question.

She blew out a frustrated breath. "Are you saying whether or not you'll help her depends on whether or not I'm her friend?"

"That's not what I'm saying. I'm just curious."

"I don't have friends. Which means I'm not *her* friend. That should work in her favor, shouldn't it?"

"That's not how the Hope Squad works. We help everyone. So, yeah, obviously I'll check on her. And not because you told me to. The Hope Squad is already aware of her."

Avery didn't seem fazed by students jostling around her as she took up residence in the middle of the hall. She blinked slowly at him before saying, "Oh yeah? You're already aware? Then what's the girl's name?"

He froze, his hands going clammy and sweaty like they always did when he was nervous.

When he didn't answer, she nodded. "That's right. You don't even know." Avery began walking backward, miraculously not running into anyone. "I think you should figure it out and do your job. I'd hate for your fans to think you're an insincere tool. A little bad publicity in a hashtag can kill a career."

She turned and was gone.

He didn't know why Avery unsettled him so much. It wasn't like she had any kind of pull in the social media world to threaten his career. He thought about what she'd said and frowned. He remembered something about a girl who'd attempted suicide awhile ago, but he didn't know any of the details.

Then he rolled his eyes at himself. It was probably that girl he'd run into, literally, just before entering the school. She'd looked pretty intensely unhappy when he saw her. He wished he would've gotten her name so he could show Avery she was wrong about him. He frowned. Not that Avery had been wrong exactly, but she certainly wasn't right. He just had a lot on his mind lately. That didn't make him a monster.

If anything, if anyone knew what he had tying up all his time, they would cut him some slack. They might even try offering him some help.

He needed a pick-me-up after dealing with his personal nemesis, so he pulled out his phone and glanced at the messages, expecting to see another proposal or two.

What he saw made him feel like someone had pumped ice into his heart.

A comment on the picture he'd just posted read, "U R such a pretender. Girl almost dies and U do what? Nothing!"

His head shot up, expecting to see Avery bent over her phone, spreading her hate for him to the online world. But he realized the message had come in when he'd been talking to Avery. She hadn't sent it. He would have said she'd put one of her friends up to leaving the comment, but she didn't have friends. She'd said so herself. She had her brother's druggie friends, but this wasn't the sort of thing they would get involved with because people like were probably distracted enough as it was.

Which meant someone else had left the comment.

But who?

He was still standing there, wondering, when the bell rang.

Addison's Journal
December 7, 8:09 a.m.

Dear Diary,

We're in the school parking lot. Mom is standing outside the car, leaning up against the door, still talking to her supervisor. She wants to say a proper goodbye to me and to give me a hug before I go in. She gave me a note to check in just in case her supervisor keeps her too long on the phone. Not that I think I'll need it. We're here early-ish, early enough for me to get to class if I run. Not that I want to go.

Yet, how do I get out of it?

No idea.

At least no ideas that wouldn't make the bags under my mom's eyes darker. And the red that rims them? That would be redder. She has cried so much. Because of me. She doesn't know that I see her cry. If I were gone, would the tears eventually dry up? Would she be able to move from this place of sad we never talk about?

She thinks I can't hear her through the door, but we drive an old 2012 Ford Focus, and the car is anything but soundproof. The seals turned brittle and died in the extreme cold of New England winters. The fact that the car is still running is its own miracle.

2012—wasn't that the year the Mayans said the world was going to end?

Mom is upset. She apparently asked for the day off as an unpaid day, but the hospital administration not only didn't grant it, they're unhappy she isn't there yet. Though she'd be there faster if they hung up and let her get on with saying goodbye to me.

Her pale-blue scrubs and yellow marshmallow winter coat are bunched against the window. The colors look happy together. Mom is like that. Happy. Even after the whole incident that brought us to Massachusetts to reboot our lives, Mom stayed happy. Or pretends it anyway. She's a lot like her hospital uniform—sanitized, bright, cheerful. The therapist asked me how I feel about my mom's way of bleaching out the bad things in our lives.

How do I feel? I don't know.

Not true. I do know.

I don't tell.

That's the difference.

* *

Avery Winters

Avery fumed as she made her way to her locker. Stupid Damion. How had she ever been friends with him? Granted, they'd been kids, but it still made her question all her life choices. She'd only tried to be nice because she'd heard some other kids throwing serious shade at him. Look where trying to be nice got her.

He didn't even know the suicide girl's name!

Most of the school had been talking about Addison Thoreau since it happened, but that pretty boy couldn't be bothered to learn the girl's name?

Seriously?

She'd been surprised to hear Addison was returning to school. Had it even been a month yet? Maybe. Either way, she didn't know if *she* would come back if her name received the same sort of vile abuse Addison's had.

Not that she really knew Addison. The only thing they had in common was that their lockers were separated by the door that was the gateway to Miss Price's rather intense literature class and one other locker that was perpetually decorated with magnets of hearts, smiley faces, and—for Christmas—Santas, elves, and manger scenes.

Avery growled in irritation. She'd seen the way that jackbag Damion had eyed her pre-algebra book and then passed judgment. What a tool. No. He wasn't just a tool. He was the whole box. No. He was the whole shed. No. He was the whole hardware store. For him to disregard her just because she wasn't rich made him the worst. Being "poor" to that overprivileged bonehead was synonymous with "stupid felon."

She wasn't stupid or a felon.

She frowned and yanked her locker open. Yet, how far off the mark had Damion hit? Didn't her brother going to jail for fentanyl possession and dealing prove his point? She clenched her jaw and shoved the pre-algebra book into the space left on the top shelf. The phone in her pocket rang, making her jump. She was going to be late for class—something that never happened. Well, never before her brother had been arrested a few weeks ago.

The phone in her pocket was his, and she was sure whoever was calling was likely a bad human. There was only one number saved on the phone, so last night, she'd sent a text with two words: *"What's up?"* She hadn't known what to expect, but now the phone was ringing. She answered because how could she find out what was really going on if she didn't answer her brother's phone? This could be the key to discovering how deep his trouble ran.

If she found people higher up on the illegal food chain, maybe she could somehow lower her brother's charges.

"Hello?"

"You're not Tyler," the voice on the other end said.

Avery wanted to say, "Well, duh," but she didn't. She simply waited for the other person to fill the silence.

"Who is this?" A girl's voice. Not a little girl, but someone not old enough to qualify as an adult either. Someone who was probably Avery's age.

"This is his sister, Avery. Tyler's not available right now, but he asked me to take his messages and take care of his people."

That was the line she'd created to maybe help "his people" feel like they could trust her.

"Do you know who I am?" the girl said.

"I know enough."

There was a mocking sort of *psh* noise on the other end. "You don't know anything. And if you don't know, then you don't need to know." There was a beep, and the phone went dead.

I'm so stupid, she thought for the millionth time since her brother had entered her room and handed her the burner phone. He had said, "Keep this safe for me. I got things going on tonight that don't feel right, and I want this safe."

He had been about to leave when she'd stopped him. "Wait. If whatever you've got going on doesn't feel right, then don't go."

"Not going would be less right." He flashed her a peace symbol and was gone.

She'd been about to go after him, to tell her dad that Tyler had been acting weird lately and that they should do something when Tyler's head had popped back around the corner.

"Dad's working late, so don't be bugging him with my problems."

"I wasn't."

He'd shot her a look that condemned her for the liar she was.

"Answer that phone if anyone calls. People are depending on me." Then he was gone.

The next time she'd seen him was when he'd been arraigned for possession with intent to distribute. He looked tired, of all things. Not scared. Not worried. Not intensely freaked out. Just tired.

Well, she was tired too. Tired of being scared. Tired of worrying. Tired of being intensely freaked out. Tired of being hung up on by some girl with unnecessary attitude.

Stupid Tyler.

Her dad refused to help raise the thousands of dollars they needed for bail money. Tyler deserved to be in jail. Her dad even said so.

Except maybe her brother didn't deserve to be in jail. They weren't those kinds of people. They were poor, sure, but poor didn't mean stupid. It didn't mean felon no matter what people like Damion Archer thought. It didn't mean reckless either.

Her brother used to hang out with guys who called themselves "the 420s"—the underbelly of the school, of the neighborhood, of the state.

But she hadn't seen him with those guys for the last couple of years. Those guys had moved on to harder criminal lives, and Tyler had moved on to something closer to normal. At least he seemed to.

He didn't have college plans, not like she did. But he'd managed to graduate high school and had been holding a steady job at Jack's Tire Repair. It was more than any of the guys who used to be his crowd could say.

Avery had been proud of how her brother had turned his life around. She was sure her mom would have been proud, too, if she'd still been alive. Tyler had spiraled into a deep depression when Mom died. She had too, but she at least tried to hold it all together. It had taken Tyler a long time, but now he was trying too. At least, she thought he was. She wished her dad could see her brother the same way she saw him.

She wished a lot of things.

"What are you doing here?"

Avery jerked her head up with the intent of snapping at whoever dared question her right to be at her own locker. But no one stood near her or was even looking in her direction. Instead, two people were standing next to Addison's locker.

It was Hazel Oliver, Addison's best friend. The other person was Booker Williams, Addison's boyfriend? Ex-boyfriend?

Honestly, Avery didn't know how he dared to even stand next to Addison's locker, not after some of the rumors she'd heard of him dumping her.

She took a deep breath and shook her head. Stupid rumors.

Stupid her for listening and judging based on stupid rumors. For all Avery knew, the breakup was Addison's idea.

Didn't she know better after everything her family, her brother, had been through?

Rumors were tidal waves in her family, crashing over them again and again.

Hazel frowned at Booker as she flipped back the box braids

of her black hair. She seemed to be listening to Booker explain his reasons for being at Addison's locker.

The pair looked awkward and uncomfortable together, and Hazel's clothes were rumpled, and she wasn't wearing any makeup. Not that Avery judged those sorts of things. People weren't clothes. People were decisions and moments. People were cause and effect.

Hazel began to cry, and Booker reached out to comfort her.

Avery was almost ashamed of watching them like they were some sort of TV drama, but she couldn't bring herself to turn away.

She had thought about approaching Addison today. She'd thought about introducing herself properly and offering friendship, but Addison had that already. Avery could tell in the way Booker and Hazel stood guard at her locker that Addison had people who cared about her. What would that be like? To have two people invested in her the way those two were invested in Addison? She'd have someone to talk to about her brother. She'd have someone to give her advice.

She'd have someone.

Several people had ridden on the coattails of Addison's ascent to fame. Infamy? They organized card signings and visits to the hospital. Avery had glared at the girl who had tried to get her to sign an oversized card with the words GET WELL SOON emblazoned on the front.

Get well soon?

What did that even mean to a girl in Addison's situation?

Avery forced herself to turn away from the drama at Addison's locker and get the books she'd needed off the second shelf.

"Would it have hurt me to sign a stupid card?" she grumbled

to herself. Would it have hurt her to carve a space where she belonged in the halls of Silver River instead of feeling like this observer she always seemed to be?

But if people wanted her to fit, wouldn't they reach out? She thought about Damion. No. They wouldn't reach out. She didn't even know why she'd bothered talking to him. Any contact they'd had over the last decade had been because she had talked to him, and he'd barely deigned to answer.

She shut her locker and made her way to class, passing the hall with Damion's locker. She shouldn't have looked—shouldn't have cared—but she did. She frowned to see him still standing there. He looked . . . vulnerable. Like the time he'd stepped on a nail, and it went through his shoe and into his foot, and he'd thought they were going to have to amputate. He'd had to lean on her as they'd hobbled together to get him home where his mom could help him.

She stepped to the side, keeping enough around the corner that he couldn't see her watching him.

He held his phone like he was confused and mortally wounded by whatever was on the screen.

She wanted to reach for him and let him lean on her shoulder like she had when they'd been kids and still friends. But she couldn't help him, could she? Hadn't this morning proved that? He always made her feel like she was nothing, even when she was trying to help him. And that's all she'd been trying to do—help.

She'd heard whispers about him as she ghosted through the halls at school. Words like *tool*, *poser*, *faker*, *narcissist*. Not that they were wrong, but they weren't right entirely either.

Damion used to pick a flower for his mom every day on the way home from school. He took the single flowers from yards with enough blooms to not be missed because he didn't want to make anyone who grew flowers sad.

Her breath caught as he turned slowly away from her, which was good because it meant she didn't have to try to hide in a near-empty hallway. He shuffle-walked like an old man with terrible burdens hanging off him like lead tethers.

She hated how her traitorous heart skipped beats as she watched him tap his phone against his thigh, creating a nervous rhythm as he trudged away from her. But why shouldn't her heart skip beats? To deny her natural attraction to his physical beauty would be a lie. Avery didn't lie.

When they were little, she'd believed they would grow up and get married someday. If only she'd known they weren't even going to grow up to be friends.

He turned the corner. She waited a moment to be certain he wouldn't come back her way before she crossed through to the next hall.

The halls were empty, and she pulled out the burner phone to check to see how late she was for class.

There was a new text from the same number that had called earlier and then hung up on her.

She opened the text to see what the angry girl had to say to her now.

"Sorry 4 hanging up. Tyler was supposed to meet me. I checked police booking website and saw he was arrested. I think my fault. We need 2 meet."

Avery's heart hammered so hard against her rib cage it felt bruised. She wanted to shout at the person on the other end, to tell them it *was* entirely their fault her brother was in jail and her father had gotten mean and stubborn.

"Who is this?" she texted back instead. She couldn't risk cutting the conversation short.

Avery caught a glimpse of Officer Whitfield at the other end of the empty hallway. She didn't want to be caught with a burner phone that belonged to her jailed brother.

She turned down the little cut-through hallway that led to the girl's restroom at the same time someone else entered from the other end. Both girls stopped when they realized they weren't alone.

Avery blinked, surprised to see Addison in front of her.

Avery tried to smile, tried to welcome this girl she didn't really know back to school, but the smile felt awkward on her face. "Hi," she said.

"Hi," Addison said back, but it took her a second to answer, as if she wasn't sure why Avery was talking to her.

They both stared at one another until Avery realized that Addison was also heading to the bathroom. She didn't look like she wanted company. She very much looked like she wanted to be alone.

"I'm going to go to class now," Avery said, pointing over her shoulder with the phone.

Addison nodded slowly. "Okay."

"But hey, um . . ." *Just spit it out,* she thought. *Say the words 'I'm glad to see you' or 'let's eat lunch together' or anything!* "I'll see you later" was all that exited her mouth.

"Right."

They both stood there for another second before Avery gave another attempt at a smile that felt all wrong on her face and left the way she'd come. As she slipped down the hallway, she felt awful that she'd been too big a coward to be a good person and welcome Addison back to school properly. Why were words hard?

The phone pinged with a new message as she walked to the back entrance of the school. *"A friend of Tyler's. Let's meet."*

The far-from-benign request did nothing to calm Avery's nerves.

She steeled herself and wrote back anyway. *"Okay. Let's meet."*

Addison's Journal
December 7, 8:31 a.m.

Dear Diary,

"I'll see you later."

A girl who has never spoken to me in my life just said that to me.

She didn't look at my arms, at my wrists. Her eyes never dropped from mine. It's possible she doesn't know who I am or what I did. But she said she'd see me later like she meant it, like I would be here later to see.

It's a lot for someone to presume right now.

And while it doesn't make sense, her saying it makes me feel like I'm obligated somehow to stick around so I can be here later to be seen.

The bell rang for class. The good news is I have a note to excuse me for being late. The bad news is I don't have a note to excuse me for anything else.

The good news is that I've got the paper done that's due today. The bad news is that I have class with Booker.

Booker.

How do I face him?

How do I explain what happened?

Booker

Booker had shown up at school early in case Addison needed help adjusting. He'd arrived before eight, which was earlier than usual for him. He wanted to make up for the fact that he hadn't been there for her. Like, at all.

Booker had wanted to visit when she was in the hospital and wanted to visit when she'd been released to go home. He'd sent a card. He'd sent flowers. He'd texted. He did not visit.

Because he wasn't sure Addison's attempt hadn't been his fault.

Addison's attempt. That was the only way he knew how to reference the whole thing. Suicide, die, kill: those words made his stomach feel like he'd eaten too much and was going to throw it all up.

He'd been the last person to see her before her attempt. And she'd run away from him as if he'd declared himself to be an alien. Part of him wondered if he was supposed to turn himself in to the police since he was the last person to see her alive.

Which was ridiculous because she was *still* alive. And he hadn't done anything wrong. But if that was true, why hadn't she said anything about the card and flowers? Why hadn't she responded to his texts?

He shifted and flinched as a locker down the hall slammed shut.

Addison wasn't there, but the gossipers were everywhere, as if they were looking for a front-row seat to whatever show Addison might provide for them. The whispers about her returning to school were on the lips of almost everyone who passed. Eyes seemed to stay on him as people realized who he was and recognized the fact that he stood in front of her locker.

Hazel, Addison's best friend, appeared at his side as if from nowhere. "What are you doing here?" she asked, her eyes narrowed and her mouth tightening into a hard slash.

"Waiting for Addison." He wanted to add *obviously* to his response, but Hazel had him pinned down with the weight of her glare.

"Did she tell you that you could be here?"

He wanted to slink away like a scolded dog. Hazel had been furious with him since Addison's attempt. A lot of people were. They blamed him because they thought he'd broken up with her. He was tired of her treating him like it was his fault. But now, seeing her up close, he saw she was as uncertain as he felt.

He leaned against Addison's locker like he owned it. "The better question is, did she tell *you* that *you* could be here?"

At that, all of Hazel's previous ice thawed into a puddle of worry and insecurity. "No," she whispered. "She won't talk to me. Is she talking to you? I mean, I'm sorry. She probably is. Of course she is. You two are so close. I just . . . Did she say anything? About me, I mean? Did she say . . ."

The girl was spiraling into a mess of panic and wide eyes. Booker put a hand on her arm to offer comfort. At his touch, she slumped against him.

"What did I do? Did she tell you? Did she say? I know I'm not the best friend in the world. I know I've neglected her a lot because of—" Her eyes flicked up the hall to where he knew Liam's locker was located. They'd been together for a while. "But she was dating you, so it's not like I abandoned her or anything. Did she say that? Did she say I abandoned her?"

Booker pulled away so he could look at her, really look at her. "So she's not talking to you?"

Hazel swallowed hard and silently shook her head as if the movement itself was a guilty verdict.

"Not at all?"

She shook her head again.

"Did she tell you why she . . . ?" But he knew immediately that Addison hadn't told Hazel why she'd made the attempt. Because if she had, Hazel wouldn't look like he felt. He had to know—had to ask. "Hazel, you don't think, you can't think . . . Do you think this is your fault?"

Her lip trembled. Tears swelled in her eyes, magnifying the blue. She was going to cry. Booker wasn't great with crying girls. The only girl in his household was his mom, and—as far as he knew—she only cried when she was happy.

"No, no, no, no, don't cry. You're okay. Honestly, I'm glad you're here."

"Why?" She sniffed. "Because I'm supposed to be her best friend, and I never called her or did anything with her and then she . . . then she . . . Why would she do this to me? Why would she try to leave me without even trying to say goodbye or tell me she was sad so I could help? Did she not think about anyone else or what it would do to them—what it would do to *me*?" Hazel took a shuddering breath, and her lip quivered.

"I don't know, but Addison's not talking to me either," he hurried to say before any of Hazel's tears could fall.

Hazel narrowed her eyes still puddled with unshed tears. "I knew it. You did break up with her."

Well, that went backward fast. Nice that he gave her the benefit of the doubt, but she wasn't willing to return the favor. "Nothing. I didn't do anything." He hoped he was telling the truth. "I don't think, anyway. But if she's not talking to you and she's not talking to me, then maybe whatever happened doesn't have anything to do with either of us. It's not your fault. And it isn't something she did to us. She has things going on that aren't about us. Emotions and grief and pain are weird. Everyone feels them differently and reacts differently."

He'd learned that from Seb. His cousin's diagnosis had sent Seb into a serious depression for one week before he was back stronger than ever and determined to fight for his life. But during that week, Seb wouldn't return calls or texts. His mom had been scared Seb might do something drastic with that depression.

He hadn't. But he'd later confided to Booker that he'd thought about it.

Booker and Hazel moved farther from each other as someone passing by whispered something about Addison's best friend stealing her boyfriend. He hated how rumors infected the school. He couldn't even stand next to Hazel without someone thinking something about it.

"Why would she shut both of us out?" she asked.

He didn't know. But he wanted to know. He wanted to help. He stood with Hazel, not so close that the gossipers could make something out of it, and waited.

Addison never showed up at her locker.

Hazel kept looking at her phone, her anxiety increasing with each glance.

"Go to class," he finally told her.

"I don't want to miss her."

"But you don't want to get into trouble either." He nudged her with his elbow. "I'll let her know you were here."

"Will you get into trouble?"

He shook his head. "It's English. I'm caught up in that class. Ms. Hall would never give me grief over being late." He wasn't sure he was telling the truth, but he smiled to show Hazel she was okay to leave her post.

Hazel nodded, glanced around—probably making sure Addison really wasn't coming—and took off to class. He'd been glad to have her standing with him. He'd felt better having someone there. With her gone, he felt exposed.

He stayed another ten minutes after the bell rang before he gave in and made his way to English. Maybe Addison was already there.

Ms. Hall greeted him with a lift of her eyebrows and a nod at the seat Booker should have been occupying. The morning had been far more anticlimactic than Booker had anticipated. It certainly hadn't been worth the night of built-up anxiety.

Addison never showed up to English.

She did make it to second-period physics four seconds before class started. She slid into her seat with barely enough time to settle her hands on her desk and her eyes on the front of the room before the bell rang.

He was sure she'd seen him—sure her eyes had fallen on him for the briefest second before they flicked away again—but she gave no indication that she'd noticed him. She could've been seeing a blank wall and given the same reaction. She didn't smile or wave or anything.

Which ticked him off.

Because he had liked Addison. He was almost certain he still did. They had always shared an easy sort of friendship. She laughed at his harebrained antics, was adequately impressed when he gave the right answers in class, and, more often than not, gave the right answers herself. They seemed evenly matched

43

when it came to course subjects. They'd been lab partners for more than one science class and in the same study group for more than one literature class. And together, they had managed to burn everything meant for a teacher's luncheon during occupational cooking.

Everything.

Well, okay, not everything. They hadn't burned the salad, but they had drowned the leaves in so much dressing that no lifeguard, coast guard, or Navy SEAL could have saved it. The cooking instructor had ordered pizza for the teachers that day.

Addison and Booker had laughed a lot.

How did that friendship count for nothing? How had that not been worth fighting for the way his cousin fought for his life?

Booker shook himself out of his thoughts. Had Mrs. O'Brien called on him to answer a question? No. Everyone had their attention turned to Valentina Rodriguez, the girl next to him. Booker breathed a sigh of relief, grateful not to get caught with his mind wandering. Especially when his mind had wandered to such a dark place.

Addison had turned slightly in her seat so she could give Valentina her attention. Booker wasn't sure, but it seemed that Addison watched him out of the corner of her eye, or at least took notice of him. But she immediately turned forward again and directed her attention to the teacher, which left Booker with a clear understanding that she did not want anything to do with him.

Fine, he thought. *I don't want anything to do with you either.* Total lie. He couldn't stop caring about her and how she was doing even if he felt so much confusion when it came to her.

Feelings weren't light switches. They didn't just turn on and off with a casual flick.

It wasn't like they could avoid each other anyway. The thing about being matched intellectually was that they shared most of their classes.

So Booker amended his earlier thought. Instead, he thought, *Fine, you think you can avoid me, but you're wrong.*

Because Booker knew one thing for certain by the time the bell rang and Addison quickly slipped from the classroom: she couldn't dodge him forever, and when the chance finally came, he meant to have a talk.

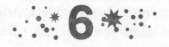

6

Addison's Journal
December 7, 9:10 a.m.

I am not writing "Dear Diary" anymore. I can't take any of this seriously if I have to write such stupid words every time I open the book.

Well, I made it to school. By that, I mean "in the building." But seriously? This was a bad idea. School, I mean. I'm not ready. I don't know what to say. I don't know how to answer the inevitable questions and looks from teachers who all know what happened. I wish I hadn't already taken my jacket to my locker because going back to get it will require me to walk past four rooms where I have class. Now that I know I can't go to those classes, it seems wrong to walk past them. Someone might see me. Though, technically, people have already seen me.

Small towns are the worst.

And okay, I know I don't really live in a small town. It's big enough to not even qualify as a town, but it's small enough that everyone knows way more than they should about their neighbors. And even with all that they know, they don't really know anything. It's staggering how invisible I am in a city of busybodies, how they can know my class schedules and test scores but know nothing about me. The actual me.

Maybe it isn't staggering. How much of their ignorance is my fault? How can they know what I never let anyone see?

I skipped my journal entry last hour. I didn't go to first hour. I needed a minute to get myself ironed out, as Mom would say. So I went into the girls' bathroom to give myself a pep talk in the mirror. I'm trying not to psychoanalyze that behavior because I'm pretty sure everyone does that. There is no need to psychoanalyze behavior that is completely pedestrian.

I really thought I was messed up, but maybe I'm not nearly as bad off as some people.

And that is not a judgment call on the girl in the bathroom. I'm actually really worried about her.

What happened was—I was writing a journal entry about that girl who told me she'd see me later, and then I was trying to do those breathing exercises and good self-talk my therapist insists will help me when I heard someone start crying in one of the stalls. I almost left. If I can't figure out my own drama, I have no business in anyone else's. Except the girl who said she'd see me later got to me.

If she can be nice, can't I do the same?

I was almost to the door when I decided to ask the crying girl if she was okay. Leaving a crying person is just not classy. She didn't answer immediately, which was a huge relief because it meant I could leave without feeling guilty, but as I wrapped my fingers around the pull handles, she said, "Not really."

Turned out it wasn't mean-girl issues or bad-boyfriend issues. It was a bizarre wardrobe issue. Not like the "I spilled spaghetti sauce on my pink top" kind of wardrobe issue, but holes. Holes in her shirt. And as soon as she said she couldn't let anyone see them, she broke into embarrassingly ugly sobbing from the other side of the stall.

I was wearing a long-sleeved shirt and a long-sleeved hoodie to cover up the mess on my arms. And I swear I could hear my therapist telling me that two is overkill—though she probably wouldn't use the word *kill*. If I'm being honest with myself and this diary, I almost left the girl anyway.

But I took off my hoodie and threw it over the stall. She was ugly sobbing so hard, what else could I do? Not gonna lie—giving it up was hard. Like "going into a room with a nuclear reactor leak without a hazmat suit" hard.

She stopped crying at least, but when she dropped her shirt to the floor, it fell outside the stall where I could see it.

The holes weren't from accidentally catching the fabric on something and ripping her shirt. They were burn marks from cigarettes. I could tell from the brown stain around each perfect, consistent circle. I asked her if she was hurting herself. I know. Like I have any right to that kind of question. But she denied it too fast to be fake. So then I asked if someone was using her as an ashtray to put out their cigarettes because seriously???

She got mad, and I left. Her monkey, her circus. If she wants to be a human ashtray, who am I to stop it?

That's the thing, though. I should've stayed. I know what it's like to have someone hurt you.

I went back, but she was gone. I checked under the stalls but didn't see any feet. I guess I'll add this on the list of things I regret. I hate how long the regret list is.

At least she's wearing my hoodie so if I see her again, I'll be able to recognize who she is. Maybe I won't choke at the chance to help someone the next time the opportunity shows up. Or maybe I'll be typically me.

Typically useless.

#whyamievenhere

Celia

Any hope Celia had of going to class vaporized with the realization that the holes looked exactly like what they were. The idiot YouTuber proved as much. Why had he called over the on-campus policeman? Why did people not mind their own business? She fled to the bathroom because where else could she go? Staying out in the parking lot would have left her to the mercy of Officer Whitfield, and as soon as he saw the burn holes, he'd call someone, and that would be disastrous. Wouldn't it?

Wouldn't it?

Fact: Celia didn't know.

She locked herself in one of the bathroom stalls and considered her options. She could run away, but then she'd lose all the benefits of her life, like the food-and-shelter thing. She could tell someone, but that would likely send her mom to jail, which would also result in the loss of food and shelter. Or she could tell and they'd send her to some foster home, which might be worse. She'd heard stories. They probably wouldn't put her in the system, though. They'd make her go live with her dad.

She shook her head.

No.

Living with her dad wasn't an option. She hardly ever saw him, hardly had any hint of him in her life aside from the Christmas cards and birthday cards and the child support he paid but that she didn't really see. Celia was pretty sure his new wife hated her. She hadn't wanted kids, but she overlooked the fact that the new husband came with a daughter since Celia's dad hadn't made it a package-deal sort of arrangement.

Celia didn't think her dad hated her, but he loved the woman who did. Fact: It was hard to forgive him for that.

What was she supposed to do? Who could she turn to?

"God, please help me," she whispered.

That was when Celia started to cry.

The sobs erupted like a volcano that had been dormant for centuries. Everything came gushing out, and Celia couldn't have stopped if she'd tried, not even when she heard a voice from the other side of her stall.

"Are you okay in there?"

When had someone else come in? How had she not heard them?

Celia's sobs stuttered, but they didn't stop. She couldn't manage to gulp in enough oxygen to even speak for several long moments—long enough that she thought maybe the other girl had left. Part of her panicked at the thought of being alone again. She needed something, someone, and she couldn't help but think that she'd asked God to help her and then this person showed up. It had to be a sign. Not that she'd expected God to answer her. He hadn't been around much in the past. But then, she'd never really talked to Him before so she couldn't exactly blame Him for anything.

"Not really," she managed to squeak out.

She thought she heard a sigh and a grunt but might have imagined it.

"What's wrong? Anything I can help with?" the girl said. "Best friend I can go get?"

Celia peered through the crack between the stall door and the wall to try to see the girl, but all she saw was a flash of brown hair and a red shirt as the girl moved from around the corner that led to the door to the hallway.

For some reason, once the girl was out of sight, it made it easier for Celia to answer. It made it easier to say aloud the thing she had only ever *almost* said aloud all those millions of times before.

"My shirt has holes!" Celia hadn't meant to wail it out like that. Her right index finger hung from one of the holes in the left sleeve.

Even though she knew her admission wasn't much, relief trickled into her soul. She'd said nothing incriminating or truly revealing, but she'd said *something*.

"Well," the girl started slowly, seeming genuinely confused by the thing Celia deemed catastrophic. "Holes can be cool, though, right?"

"No!" Celia said. Another wail. Why couldn't she speak without it coming out in foghorn bursts? "I can't go to class with my shirt like this. I can't let anyone see me."

"Why don't you just go home and change your clothes?"

"No!" Anxiety spiked in Celia, turning her wail into a frantic shriek. "I . . . I can't. I just c-can't."

Seconds passed. Maybe minutes. Celia didn't know. It felt like a long time. She hung her head in shame over how stupid she was acting. The pale-sand-and-gray floor tiles made patterns that distracted her for a bit of that time. She could almost make faces out of those tiles if she squinted hard enough.

Fact: You could see a face in about anything if you looked long enough.

"I . . ." The girl made a noise that sounded as if she was swallowing hard, as if she wasn't certain she could say what she was going to say. "I have something you can wear if you want. I probably overdressed for the day. Do you want it?"

Celia thought about the burn marks on her arm. If the girl

gave her a short-sleeved shirt, people would still see the bandages on her skin. It didn't matter; the gift offered was not one she could turn down.

"Are you sure?"

Instead of responding, the girl simply threw a wad of red cloth over the top of the stall. Celia caught it automatically.

The cotton hoodie had obviously been ironed by somebody that morning, probably the girl, maybe her mom. Ironed clothing. Who even did that anymore?

Celia didn't think her mother even owned an iron, and she was glad of that. It was one less thing she had to worry about her mother using against her. *Stop that,* she thought. Her mother had never burned her before, not once before the cigarette disaster. And that hadn't been her. That had been her boyfriend.

Celia shook her head, trying not to think about all the different things that led her to this moment. What mattered was getting something safe to wear, and someone had done that for her.

Before she lost herself in overthinking everything, like she always did, Celia stripped off the shirt with the burn marks. She would throw it away here at school, where her mother wouldn't be able to find it in the garbage and pull it back out again.

"Are those cigarette burns?" the girl on the other side of the stall asked.

Celia looked down to see her white shirt on the floor outside the stall. In her effort to throw the thing away from herself, she hadn't been careful enough.

She snatched it back up, rolled it into a ball, and put it on top of the small metal trash can hooked to the side of the bathroom stall. "It's nothing."

"Girl, you're in a bathroom, crying, and your shirt has

cigarette burns in it. That's definitely something. Are you . . . hurting yourself?"

"No!" Celia shouted, furious anyone could even think that.

"Okay. No," the girl said. And then, after a moment, she added gently, "You're not a human ashtray, you know. And if someone's using you as one, that's totally messed up. If those really are cigarette burns, you need to tell someone."

"This really isn't any of your business. So just let it go."

"Fine, you want me to let it go? I can go. But the free advice came with the free shirt. I don't actually care what you do with either one. But if those holes aren't what I think they are, well then, you wouldn't be getting so defensive, would you? You have a right to protect yourself."

The girl on the other side of the stall actually sounded mad. Then the door of the bathroom banged against the wall as if the girl had yanked on the handle as hard as she could. The door settled closed again much more quietly than it had opened.

But Celia wasn't sure the girl had gone. "Hello?"

She waited but received nothing but silence. "Hello? Are you still there?"

Whoever the girl had been, she was gone now. Celia, not knowing what else to do, slid her arms into the sleeves and pulled the hoodie over her head. It was probably the first time in her life she had worn a top that wasn't wrinkled in some way.

She used to hang her clothing in the bathroom so the steam would pull some of the wrinkles out of the fabric. But then her mother had smacked her with one of the hangers. The shirt had still been hanging from the metal hanger when her mom went at her with it, which meant the cloth had provided a small buffer against her skin, so it wasn't so bad.

Her mother's shrill voice had bounced off the walls of the

hallway where she'd encountered Celia holding the many hangers of various clothing. She yelled about how tacky it was to have clothing hanging on the shower curtain rod where anyone could see. Her mother had screamed, "Haven't I taught you better than that?"

Fact: Her mother had never mentioned hanging clothes in the bathroom before that moment.

Celia learned to get used to the wrinkles after that. No reason to poke the bear if she didn't need to.

The soft cotton against her skin felt comforting. Celia wondered if she was supposed to give the hoodie back. Except, who would she give it back to? She didn't know anything about the girl.

But the girl knew something about her.

The girl had told her to tell someone. She had called Celia's life *messed up*.

She wasn't wrong. Celia knew that. Hadn't Celia wanted to tell someone a million times?

So why did she feel so angry that someone confirmed what she already knew? And was she angry at the girl? How wrong was that? A perfect stranger *literally* handed her the shirt off her back, and Celia had the nerve to be angry at her?

Messed up.

Was it Celia's *life* that was messed up, or was it *Celia* who was messed up? She didn't know. She didn't know how to separate herself from the life she lived.

She took several deep, long breaths and finally got the nerve to exit the stall.

She half expected the girl to be leaning against the tiled wall, waiting for her. But the bathroom was empty. She didn't know if she was grateful to find herself alone, or sad. Part of her had wanted somebody to step in and force her to do the thing she didn't think she was brave enough to do.

But no one was there to force her to do anything. She looked in the mirror; the red of the hoodie matched the red rimming her eyes. Somehow that was comforting in a twisted way Celia didn't understand.

Wrapping her arms around herself, Celia felt the burn inside the crook of her elbow. That one had been the worst, and it was in a place where it was harder to keep covered with a bandage. Anywhere the body bent was hard to bandage.

When she heard the bell announce the end of class, she retreated to the safety of the locked stall, sat cross-legged on the toilet so her feet wouldn't show, and listened as people came and went from the bathroom.

She waited until the bell herded people back to class, until the bathroom was empty again. She stayed there a long time, holding the burned shirt in her hands, wringing it and wringing it as if she could force out the burn marks.

She finally stood, opened the stall, and threw the shirt in the garbage can. Then she pulled out paper towels—lots of them. She kept tugging them out, wadding them up, and jamming them into the garbage until the shirt was buried so deep no one would go digging for it.

Celia took another deep breath, gave herself a final stern look in the mirror, and turned and left the bathroom. She didn't know where she was going until she stood in front of the school office. When she pulled open the door, it finally occurred to her what she intended to do.

Terror settled into her bones, making her hand tremble against the door handle.

What am I doing? The cold metal warmed until it felt like it might burn her palm. *I can't do this. What will happen to me if I take the next step?*

But she did take the next step—almost without wanting to, almost without making the decision herself.

The door was open, and she crossed the threshold into the office—the first step to something that, she hoped, would be better.

7

Addison's Journal
December 7, 10:07 a.m.

It turns out I was right to worry—I've been assigned as some-one's project. A famous online celebrity goes to our school, and practically everyone is in love with him. He *is* attractive, but he's not *Booker* attractive.

There's a lot of charm and whatever it is that draws people to people oozing off Damion Archer. But there is something so much more attractive about the quiet way Booker is.

He tugs at the hair behind his ears when he's studying or worry-ing or just absentmindedly looking at something. His coils are actu-ally pretty long, and when he pulls on them, they spring back into place. He doesn't tug hard or anything, so it's not like some weird self-harming ritual. It's just a gentle pull. I've watched him do that for years.

I always thought I would get a chance to stretch out one of those curls. I always thought we'd get close enough to allow that kind of touching.

That chance is lost to us now. How did we get to this place?

I feel like if I look down at my hands, they will be bloodied—cut from all the shattered fragments of me that I'm trying to hold together. Booker is just another bit of broken glass.

I used to think my high school was huge, that it was a place where you could get lost in the anonymity of the crowd, but it turns out avoiding someone in that crowd is hard when he's in most of my classes.

I wonder if the therapist will read this journal.

Will she ask me to hand it over and then pick apart every word? What will she say about the Booker question?

· ·

Damion

Damion decided to run an investigation regarding the girl Avery had mentioned. When he checked his phone after his last two classes, he found many new messages calling him out for not being a better part of the Hope Squad and for not caring about students in general—for being a fraud and a faker and undeserving of his fame. It was as if someone had started a campaign against him.

He needed to figure out the girl's name and her schedule so he could meet up with her, introduce himself, and then maybe eat lunch with her or walk her to class or offer to help her in some way. He needed to do something where people saw him with her so the hater comments and direct messages could stop.

The direct messages were the worst of them and all from fake accounts. He'd been involved in social media long enough to know the difference between fake and legit accounts. Some fake accounts were smoother than others, but the ones who DM-ed him about how he didn't deserve his fame and that he was a shallow hack who didn't care about anyone except himself weren't even trying to hide their fakeness. It was like they had been waiting for him to slip up about something so they could unleash this frenzied cyber-mob attack. The whole Hope Squad thing was just the excuse they'd chosen to use.

But they *were* using it.

He should do a video about internet anonymity turning what might have been perfectly ordinary, nice humans into mutants. Not anytime soon, obviously, lest the current haters decide to make their messages public, but sometime in the future.

He did a quick check at the front office to see if Chloe was around. That girl knew everything happening in the school, and he was pretty sure she liked him, at least enough to tell him what he needed to know.

Chloe wasn't working the office, though.

He would have checked with someone in the Hope Squad, except he didn't know where the messages were coming from. No reason to fuel that fire in case it was an inside job. He had to figure this out on his own. As he stood in the foyer that led to the back door, he looked toward the expanse of frosted-over lawn and saw someone who gave him an idea: Avery Winters.

Avery had a phone in her hand and was pacing in circles, her breath puffing out in clouds of white vapor. He pushed the bar on the glass door and walked out to join her, the grass crunching under his feet. He wished he had his coat, but he couldn't turn back now because Avery had already seen him, and she wasn't wearing one. At least they hadn't had any snow yet.

She stuffed the phone in her pocket and stared at him, her face unreadable, as he approached.

"Hey, Avery."

She raised her eyebrows. "Using my actual name instead

of calling me *Frosty Winters*? Wow. You must have had a tough morning."

The comment made him doubt himself. What if *she* had been the one to create those fake accounts and send those messages? Trusting her with the fact that she'd been right about him might be his biggest mistake ever. He did an inward eye roll. Avery might not like him, but she wasn't a vindictive shrew.

"I'm coming to you to confess."

She scoffed. "I'm not your pastor, Archer, so you can move along." She waved her hand to shoo him away.

He didn't move. "I don't know the girl's name."

She tilted her head to look up at him. It was weird to think they used to be the same height and always able to see eye to eye. "That is an unexpected confession," she said.

"If I'm being fully honest, as I suspect one should when confessing anything, it's unexpected for me as well."

She waited for the space of three puffs of frozen air to escape her before saying, "What am I supposed to do with that information?"

He shrugged. "I was hoping you would tell me her name and enough about her to find her so I can do some actual good around this place."

"Why would I do that?"

"Because you're a good person and you want to see the girl get whatever she needs to be okay."

Avery's cheek twitched as she looked down at the frozen grass. He'd forgotten about that little twitch that happened as part of her frown. She let out a deep breath. "You don't think I'm a good person."

He laughed. "You mean *you* don't think *I'm* a good person. Let me show I can be."

"Fine. But if I do this for you, you need to do something for me."

He shifted, uncomfortable with the idea of owing her a favor. He hesitated, but when his phone buzzed with a new message that was possibly—probably—toxic, he hurried to say, "Okay. Sure. What do you need?"

"I have to meet someone during first lunch, but I don't want to go alone. Do you have first lunch?"

"Avery, I don't do fan meet and greets."

She shoved him with the heel of her hand. "Get over yourself, princess. This isn't that kind of favor. I just need you to wait in the car while I meet with someone. Just answer the question. Do you have first lunch?"

If he felt wary before, he was downright terrified now. "Yes, I do, but I'm not going to be the getaway car while you knock over a convenience store or do a drug deal."

She threw her hands up in the air. "You know what? Just forget it." She turned, tucked her hands under her arms, and stalked back to the school.

"Whoa, whoa, whoa!" He slipped on the icy grass, trying to catch up to her as he caught her wrist to keep her from making an angry exodus.

She jerked out of his loose grasp and turned on him with a glare hot enough to melt the entire state out of its winter. "Do *not* touch me, Archer."

He lifted his hands in surrender. "Sorry. I'm sorry. About all the things. It's just important for me to know what I'm getting myself into. If you can vouch for the legality of our actions and ensure I won't be mobbed by weird fans, then fine. Whatever. I'm in."

Her frown deepened, which was not the reaction he expected to his willingness to help.

She finally nodded. "Her name is Addison Thoreau. Her locker is near mine. On the other side of Miss Price's classroom door and right next to a locker that has Santa and manger scene magnets on it." She nodded again and walked away.

He let her get far enough ahead to keep her from feeling like he was following her, and then he headed back as well, glad to get out of the cold and glad to have some direction. He checked his phone. There were only four minutes left of the break before class. Was he going to be late for everything today?

He immediately went to Miss Price's classroom, saw the locker with the Christmas décor, and then realized someone was at the locker Avery had indicated. The girl moved like a phantom. He almost missed her entirely. He had to hurry before she got away.

"Hey, Addison."

The girl looked up and seemed surprised to see him standing in front of her, which surprised him. He assumed someone from the Hope Squad had told her to expect a visit, but, really, what did he know about it? He missed most of the meetings. He wasn't entirely sure what the Hope Squad did or didn't do.

"Hi, I'm Damion Archer, and—"

"I know who you are," Addison said.

"Oh. Well. Good. And I know who you are as well. And I thought I'd stop by and see if you needed anything or if there was anything I could get for you or whatever." He sounded asinine, even to his own ears. He spent enough time editing his own work to know when he needed a recording do-over. Sadly, real conversation didn't allow do-overs.

She held his gaze. "Did they send you to deal with me?" she finally asked.

He felt surprised she would ask such a point-blank question.

"No one sent me. I'm here because I want to be here."

"Well, don't worry about it—about me. I'm fine."

Wow, that was unexpected. He hadn't anticipated an outright rejection of his help. He glanced around the halls and noticed that for the first time in forever, nobody was noticing him. He needed people to see him with her. He hated himself for thinking such a thing even as he said, "You probably are fine. I mean you look fine." His face flushed hot. "I mean not that you look fine in the 'I'm trying to harass you' kind of way but in a general sense of the word." He blew out a deep breath. "Look, I'm not really any good at this. If I'm being honest, and I kind of have to be since you're here as a witness, I really suck at this. But I really do want us to be friends. No strings, just friends. Can I walk you to class?"

She gave him a look like she'd eaten something unexpected and slightly unpleasant. It reminded him of the first time he ever tasted sauerkraut. That was also the last time he had ever tasted sauerkraut. He hoped he managed to leave a better impression for her than sauerkraut had for him.

"Sure," she said. "Why not? But if you make me late . . ."

She left that comment hanging in the air.

"We'll speed walk." He fell into step next to her, and she really did speed walk, at least until it looked like she'd not only be to class on time but she might also be early.

"So no one sent you, huh?" she asked, suddenly wanting to make conversation in spite of the fact she'd shrugged off his every attempt to get to know her better.

"No one sent me. Cross my eyes."

She slowed to a stop and stared at him for a moment. "You mean cross my heart?"

"I'm pretty sure crossing my heart would lead to important arteries getting tangled and blood supply suffering. It's physically impossible. I prefer to cross my eyes."

"You're funny. I didn't know that about you."

Clearly she'd never watched any of his videos because if she had, she'd know he was hilarious.

"I'm only funny to people with a good sense of humor, which tells me a little something about you."

She frowned. "What could that possibly tell you? Nobody really knows anything about me. I sometimes wonder if *I* know anything about me."

Out of his peripheral, he noticed her fingers curl up and slip into her sleeves. She tugged them lower over her wrists before bringing her arms up to cross them protectively over her chest.

The motion of her fingers tugging her sleeves shifted something in him—something like worry. Worry for something outside his sphere? That was new. He suddenly wanted to help her for her sake, not for his.

"Funny people are generally observed to be the best-loved. I mean, generally. This means you are the rare kind of person who will live a long life filled with the kind of love that guarantees you will be remembered."

Her chin lifted in a way that was not unlike Avery when he'd offended her.

"Wow." She let out a small laugh. "Did that come straight out of that stupid Hope Squad manual or something?"

"No," he said, slightly bristling. "*This* came straight out of a Hope Squad manual: 'A Harvard study found that nine out of ten people who attempt suicide and survive don't make a second attempt.' I thought it was interesting that the majority of suicide survivors don't attempt again, which is why I remember it. What I said before came from me because I like people with a sense of humor. My mom is funny, and she's one of the best people I know." They stood in front of a classroom door, but Addison made no move to go inside. He kept talking. "You seem like a cool person, and I just think it's important that cool people know that they're cool. That's all."

"Okay. But what you said before was wrong. Living a long life is all fine and good. But it isn't about the people who re-member you when you're gone. It's about who you remember while you're here. It's about who is occupying *your* mental space. Thanks for walking me to class."

She slipped into the classroom quickly and quietly just as the bell clamored through the halls. He felt pretty certain he stood there, slack-jawed, for several moments.

How could she have known to say exactly that?

Then he grunted. She'd made it to class on time, but he wouldn't. Obviously.

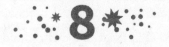

Addison's Journal
December 7, 11:11 a.m.

The time is inspiring. All those ones lined up in a row on the digital clock on my teacher's desk. One. The chosen one. It all comes down to one. One and only. Once and for all. Once upon a time . . .

Once upon a time is a thing of fairy tales. But anyone who's read the Brothers Grimm or Perrault or Hans Christian Andersen knows that those stories are messed up and far closer to ugly reality than happily ever after.

Why do I keep coming back to this? I've got to stop obsessing. It didn't start with Booker. I know that. Intellectually, I know that. Emotionally? I don't know anything emotionally.

I've been thinking about what the famous kid said. Through the whole of my last class and now into this one. About the Harvard study. Nine out of ten people who attempt suicide don't attempt it again. They go on to live happy, good lives. Okay, he hadn't said happy or good, but they went on to live. Doesn't it stand to reason that they were happy? That they did some good somewhere? Why else would they stay?

I know he was being glib when he said it—but he got to me. I hadn't expected he could do that on a walk that took what—three minutes?

The question I need to ask now is, am I part of the nine, or am I the one?

. . . .

Avery

Avery's leg bounced like it was having its own personal earthquake as she watched the clock on the wall above Mr. Ferris's head. The guy looked like Morgan Freeman a little, minus the soothing voice. She hardly heard her gray-haired science teacher's lecture about the periodic table and atomic numbers and why it all mattered.

It didn't matter. Not to her. Not at that moment. The only thing that had any importance in her life was that clock and the hands that moved her closer to . . . well, she didn't know what exactly, but to something.

And then it happened. The hands moved to the first lunch position. People were getting up, gathering their stuff, and leaving. She leaped up and maneuvered her way through the crowd and managed to get out the door before anyone else. From there, she dashed to meet Damion.

When she turned the corner to find no one at her locker, she let out a long, disappointed-but-not-surprised breath. Tool jackbag Damion! Part of her also felt relieved by his absence. What if she ended up involved in something not exactly legal? She'd told Damion everything was on the up-and-up, but what if she was wrong? Her brother sat in jail, and she was pretty sure he hadn't gotten there by sending flowers to nice little old ladies. If Damion flaked, he wouldn't be able to witness her digging herself into the same hole as her brother. She did not need witnesses to her stupidity. She would do this by herself.

She jerked open her locker, stuffed in her books with a growl, and pulled out her motorcycle keys.

"It's Avery, right?"

The small female voice made her drop her keys and bang her elbow against her open locker door. She gave a tiny yip of pain and rubbed her funny bone before she registered who had spoken.

Addison Thoreau.

"Right. Hi." She felt like her jaw might be dragging on the floor as she stared at Addison. She made an effort to close her mouth and work it into something she hoped would be taken as a smile.

"I just wanted to say thanks . . . for earlier."

Thanks? What would Addison possibly have to thank her for? The question must have been evident on her face because Addison said, "You just said something that got me thinking in a way I haven't been thinking for a long time, and, anyway, I just wanted to say thank you."

Avery reached back to try to pull any memory of any conversation she might have had with Addison to warrant a verbal offering of gratitude.

She couldn't think of anything.

"You're welcome?" She hated that it sounded like a question. She hated that she felt inconvenienced by this girl reaching out to her right at the moment when she needed to leave.

"Well, anyway . . ." Addison's face flushed a slight pink. She backed up a step and looked like she had every intention of leaving when Damion's radio-personality voice called out.

Avery glanced down the hall to see Damion waving.

"You're friends with Damion?" Addison asked.

"We were. A long time ago. We've kind of been fighting for almost a decade."

"You don't look like you're fighting. Did you guys make up or something?"

Avery laughed and shook her head. "Not likely. Maybe we'll think about being friends at some point in the future, but it certainly isn't going to happen today."

Addison shrugged. "What's the old saying? 'Next year, you'll wish you started today' or something like that?"

Avery wanted to respond, but Damion had closed the distance between them.

He smiled at Addison as he tucked himself to the side to keep from getting run over by hall traffic. "Hey, Addison. What's up?"

Damion's casual way of talking to people grated on Avery. He didn't seem to feel uncomfortable at all around the girl the way Avery did. He was all calm and irritatingly Damion-Archer-famous.

"You're here?" Avery couldn't have kept the surprise out of her voice if she'd wanted to.

"As promised."

Addison pointed down the hall. "Well, I gotta go. Thanks again. And thanks to you too, Damion. I appreciate you talking to me earlier."

Damion shifted his backpack strap and held out his hands in an invitation. "You don't have to go. You can come with us."

Avery wanted to slap that offer right off his mouth. Seriously? Was he serious right now? He'd gone from asking Avery if she was doing a drug deal or knocking over a convenience store to inviting other people as if he were selling tickets to a theme-park attraction?

Her mind raced for ways to uninvite Addison without making her feel unwelcome when Addison said, "I have class right now, not lunch. But thanks. Really. Thanks." Addison looked down and frowned before picking something up off the floor. "It looks like you dropped something. At least I'm assuming it's yours since it has your name on it."

She handed what appeared to be a thin wooden bookmark to Damion, whose mouth opened and closed several times in silence as he took it from her.

He cleared his throat. "Thanks. I don't know how that got out of my backpack. Thank you."

Was Damion's voice trembling? Why did he sound like he might start crying?

Avery glanced at the bookmark. It had his name on it, which made her want to laugh because seriously? He was getting all choked up over his name on a piece of wood? Ego much?

She didn't make fun of him, though. She remembered how vulnerable he'd looked earlier that morning when he'd been basically alone in the hallway. He had stuff he was dealing with, and even if she didn't understand what or why, she could respect that stuff was stuff. Everyone's stuff looked easy on the outside. Inside was another thing altogether.

While Avery had been lost in her own thoughts, Addison disappeared into the crowd. Avery felt like a serious jackbag for not saying goodbye or being helpful to the girl who clearly had her own stuff.

"I suck," she muttered.

"What?"

"Nothing," she said, realizing she'd spoken aloud. "Let's go."

She led the way to the student parking lot and then turned to where she'd parked her motorcycle.

When she began unlocking the helmets, Damion held out his hands in protest. "Whoa. Seriously? No. This is a huge helping of never-gonna-happen with a side dish of nope."

"I'm a good driver. We're perfectly safe."

"And cold. It's winter, Avery *Winters*. In case you hadn't noticed."

"We're not going that far."

"Great. Then I'll drive." He sauntered off, leaving Avery with no real choice except to lock up the helmets and follow him.

Once they were in his black Honda Accord, she gave him the address for the GPS, put on her seat belt, and settled in. She sneaked a peek at Damion as he pulled onto the road. "I'm surprised," she finally said.

"Over?"

"This car. I expected . . . something else."

"What? Like a sports car, something bright yellow with a neon sign that flashes 'Look at me' every so often?"

She cringed. "Sorry. That's pretty judgy of me, isn't it?"

"Yes. But we'll call it fair play since I basically accused you of dealing drugs earlier."

She cringed again but hoped he didn't notice. She had no idea who she was meeting, and she wouldn't have agreed to an in-person meeting except the voice on the other end of that phone call had sounded . . . not scary. But not *sounding* scary didn't mean not *being* scary.

She peeked again at Damion. He could call for help if things went bad. And if things went well, maybe she would have some clue about how to help her brother.

When they arrived at the address, Damion glanced at the

sign above the building and raised an eyebrow at her. "A coin-op laundromat?"

"What?"

"You gonna tell me what this is all about, or do you really think I'm dumb enough to believe you're switching out your laundry?"

Avery huffed. "Just stay in the car. If I'm not back out in ten minutes, call for help."

"Help as in police?"

"No!"

Both of his eyebrows went up.

"Maybe. Just wait here." She got out of the car and wondered if he really would wait. She wasn't sure she would if the roles were switched.

She stepped over the crumbled sidewalk and opened the laundromat door. Rusted bells hanging from a string that might have been red once but had faded to a nondescript gray jangled her presence to whoever was inside.

Avery frowned. The only other person inside was a young, fair-skinned woman with a baby strapped to her front in a baby backpack. She rocked back and forth to the uneven beat of what sounded like shoes tumbling inside a nearby dryer. Great. The whole meeting was probably a bust.

Avery turned to leave. She'd wait outside in Damion's car. Ten minutes. The girl she was supposed to meet would get ten minutes before Avery directed Damion to head back to school.

The bells jingled again as she moved to exit when the woman with the baby called out. "Are you Tyler's sister?"

Avery stopped and slowly turned back to the woman with the baby. No. Not woman but girl. She couldn't have been any older than Avery. Her dark hair was tied back with a ponytail holder, and her brown eyes darted around to make sure Avery stood alone.

Had the girl really brought a baby to a meeting that required a burner phone to set up?

"Okay?" Avery answered, not entirely sure what she meant by that answer.

The baby started to fuss once the girl stopped rocking to the beat. She began swaying again. Maybe she wasn't the mom. Maybe she was just babysitting.

"I'm Avery."

The girl smiled. "I'm Jo. And this is Tyler."

Jo looked down at the baby with a smile that definitely called her out as the mother and—

Avery was sure her eyes had never been so wide. "Wait a minute. Your baby's name is Tyler? Like my brother?"

"Like his father."

Avery liked to think she wasn't stupid in spite of what people like Damion thought of her, but it took her a moment to puzzle those pieces together. "You and Tyler—the tall one, not this infant one—are dating?"

She shrugged. "For a couple of years now."

"And you have a kid." Her dad was not going to love that news when it came out. "And you didn't tell anyone."

Jo hesitated like she was trying to find the best way to explain. "We thought it would be safer that way."

"Safer?"

"My brother really hates your brother. They worked for competing employers."

"By employers you mean dealers."

She bit her lip but nodded. As if by instinct, she took the baby's hand in her own and rubbed her thumb over his tiny fingers. "So, the baby's name on the birth certificate is Ethan. And I call him Ethan whenever anyone else is around, but when it's just me, I make sure my little boy knows who he is. I just have to be careful, see? If my brother finds out about us, it'll be bad."

Avery considered herself a pretty open-minded person. She thought she had a good hold of reality and understood the stupid things people did, but this was beyond what she'd expected. She'd come hoping to find evidence that her brother had been wrongfully arrested. She hadn't expected to find that not only did her idiot jackbag brother deserve to be behind bars but he'd also left a kid behind.

"I'm sorry," Avery said. "Bad as in worse than my brother being in jail?"

"It was my brother who told the police where and when to find Tyler. He doesn't like competition, so he got rid of it. If Jace finds out that Tyler and I are together, I don't know what he'll do."

Avery processed the information before saying, "Okay. Before we continue with this"—she waved her hand between them—"whatever this is, I need to know something. Is my brother guilty? Did Tyler really intend to distribute?"

Jo nodded.

Avery wanted to throw up. She wanted to hit something. Someone. She wanted to— "So all your brother did was tell the truth?"

Jo nodded again and began bouncing the baby with a little more energy.

So. There would be no getting her jackbag brother out of jail for wrongful arrest or on some plea deal because she could give the cops information on a bigger thug. Her brother was guilty, and now there was this girl and her baby. "I don't get it. Why the burner phone? Why the secret meeting? Why all the drama?"

"If Jace sees me with a member of Tyler's family, he'll freak. I just don't think I can keep my baby safe."

How many more ways could Avery's mind shift? From judgment to irritation to anger to fear for the two people in front of her. "So what do we do?" Just like that, they were a *we*.

"I need a place to stay. A place where Jace won't look. I hoped . . . Well, if I stayed at your house in Tyler's room while Tyler's in jail, Jace won't think about that. No one would know."

"My dad would know." All the insulation in the world could not keep her dad from hearing a baby crying.

"We'll stay out of the way."

Jo's wide, desperate eyes made Avery feel like a jerk for asking her next question. "How do I feed you?"

Everyone in their household did their own thing. Everyone pretty much paid for their own individual needs. Her dad paid the utility bills and property taxes. There was no mortgage thanks to the modest life-insurance policy her mom had left behind. It wasn't much but enough to pay off the small home. Other than that, they all made their own way without getting in each other's way—each of them absorbed in their own personal grief over the loss of her mother.

"I don't have any money. That's why Tyler was doing that last job. He was gonna get the payout, and we'd all go somewhere else. Somewhere warmer. Be a family." She smiled at the idea but then frowned as if remembering her dreams were behind bars and she didn't have any way to pay for herself.

The bells jingled again, making both Avery and Jo jump and whirl to face the newcomer.

"Damion!" Avery shouted when she saw him. "What are you doing?"

"It's been ten minutes." He looked confused by the rather innocuous scene in front of him.

In all honesty, she'd forgotten about him. "You were supposed to call for help, not crash in here. What if I'd been doing something dangerous?"

"You said you weren't doing anything dangerous. And what kind of help could I call without assessing the situation? Ambulance? Police? Coast guard? Dogcatcher?"

He had a point.

"I was just meeting up with my brother's girlfriend and my nephew." She glanced at the baby. She had a nephew. That tidbit would require some emotional unraveling. "Would you be willing to do me a favor?"

His gaze passed from her to the baby and back again, and his eyebrows shot up as if to remind her he was still in the middle of the first favor.

"I know. I know. But I just need you to drive us all back to my house. Jo's going to stay with me for a while."

Avery looked at the time left on the dryer and *tsk*ed. There was no way to wait for Jo's clothes, drive to her house, and get Damion back to school in the amount of time left in the lunch break.

"Those aren't mine," Jo said as she followed Avery's gaze.

Avery glanced around. No one else was in the laundromat with them. "Someone left their clothes here?"

Jo shrugged, her brown ponytail brushing her shoulder.

Avery wouldn't have trusted that no one would steal her stuff, but maybe the owner had more faith in humanity than she did.

To Damion's credit, he didn't ask why Jo was hanging out in a laundromat when she didn't have clothes in a machine. He *did* ask about a car seat and was visibly relieved when Jo produced said car seat and a duffel bag from behind a bunch of worn chairs next to the washers.

He also asked Jo some get-to-know-you questions as he helped her hook the car seat in. Avery hadn't thought about a car seat. She hadn't thought to ask Jo anything about herself beyond the initial shakedown for information regarding her brother.

"I suck," she muttered.

"Stop saying that," Damion said softly to her.

She rolled her eyes at herself. She'd said it loud enough for him to hear. Again, apparently. But it mattered to her that he wasn't agreeing with her, that he seemed so much more comfortable now that he knew she hadn't tangled him up in something illegal. She squeezed her eyes shut to block out the anxiety she felt. She couldn't get sucked into a mental breakdown when she had so much to deal with already.

During the drive to Avery's house, Damion's questioning skills taught Avery a lot about Jo. She learned that Jo and Jace had been raised by a rather strict and angry aunt. She learned the aunt had kicked them out when Jace turned twenty-one, insisting Jace was old enough to take care of his little sister. She learned that Jo was nineteen years old, which was a good three years older than Avery had thought. She learned that little Tyler was four months old and that he liked it when his dad sang to him. Up to that point, Avery hadn't known Tyler ever sang.

Damion pulled up in front of her house. He helped unload the car seat with the baby and hefted it into the house.

"Thanks," Avery said after walking him back out and watching him get in his car.

"No worries. It's the least I could do after you tried to warn me that people were trashing on me."

"You know, it shouldn't matter to you what they say about you."

He hunched his shoulders slightly. "Except it does."

"Why?"

"It's a long story, Avery."

She stood there awkwardly with his open car door between them before she realized she had no reason to keep him longer. She nodded, shut the door, and waved him on.

Then she turned to face her house and the new situation that waited for her inside.

Addison's Journal
December 7, 11:42 a.m.

My therapist explained something to me that I'd never understood before. She said that people don't show enough gratitude for the little things. She started me on a gratitude journal way before I started this whole epic journal thing.

The journal was a little notebook that fit in my pocket. I was to pull it out anytime something happened that was good—even if it was a small good, like crunchy peanut butter or whatever. I didn't have to write details or anything, just the word, the one word of whatever it was. It was really more of a list than a journal. At least in the beginning.

It started out with inanimate objects. I had butterflies and beach glass and flyswatters and the Freedom Trail manhole covers all on that list. Then I started taking pictures of those things with my phone—kind of like photo evidence of good things. At night, I scrolled through the images and repeated in my head the words I'd written. They were things to live for.

I don't know why, but it took me some time before people ever showed up on the list. My mom deserved to be the first thing I wrote down. But she wasn't. I didn't.

I don't know what that means.

It took me awhile to realize I never said thank you. To anyone. For anything of importance. Not really.

Sure, I thank cashiers when they hand back change, and I thank people who hold doors open for me. I thank my mom for making me toast with apple butter.

But the real kind of thanks? I don't do that.

I didn't thank my mom for believing me when I told her the truth all those years ago. I didn't thank her for taking me and running away so I wouldn't get hurt again. I didn't thank her for the right things. Not like I should have. I still haven't thanked her. It's one more thing I don't do well.

But after talking to the therapist, I've decided it's important to say thank you when you have the chance. You never know when there won't be chances later. I said thanks to the girl who said she'd see me later. She seemed confused, but it made me feel better to say it out loud to her. My therapist is right. It would suck to owe someone a thank-you and hold it unsaid in your mouth. The bitter taste of unsaid words leaves cankers. I should know. I have a lifetime of unsaid words stored up.

Booker

Celia Cameron walked into the office. Booker only knew who she was because he'd tutored her in math class back in ninth grade. He was pretty sure she'd still failed, and he still felt bad about that. She was quiet enough that she was easy to overlook. But after having spent time with her, he knew that what she lacked in math skills, she made up for in other areas where she was obviously a million times smarter than he was.

He also knew there were things obviously wrong in her life.

Even if he hadn't already suspected her home life sucked, the way Janice, the office secretary, seemed both alarmed and thrilled to have Celia standing in front of her would have clued him in.

"Hello, Celia," Janice said with her lilting Spanish accent. She had the entire school student body memorized. She knew their birthdays, and probably even their favorite candy bars. Booker believed a memory like that deserved to be highlighted on a game show, not wasted in a high school front office. She could probably win millions. He'd once brought it up to her, and she'd laughed at him.

Booker sometimes wondered if what Janice knew went beyond names, birthdays, and possible candy bar preferences because she had a way of looking at him like she knew more than she told. She looked at everyone that way. And now she was looking at Celia that way.

He would've gotten back to sorting mail for the teachers' boxes except something caught his eye.

Celia's shirt. She wore a long red pullover hoodie. He didn't notice because it was cool or because it looked good on her. He noticed it because it wasn't hers. It was Addison's.

While he knew it wasn't outside the realm of possibility that both girls had similar hoodies, it wasn't just similar. It was the exact same.

He was sure because Addison had been wearing it the time they'd hiked to Tucker Brook Falls in New Hampshire. There had been snow along the trail, and the small bridge had been icy enough that Booker had slipped and fallen in the water. Addison had panicked, but once she realized he was just soaked and not hurt, she'd laughed. When she'd leaned over to help him up, she'd caught her hoodie on a nail. It had left a small tear in the bottom.

The same tear was in the hoodie Celia wore.

He looked down at the papers in his hands and moved more slowly so he had an excuse to hang around and figure out why Celia was wearing Addison's clothing.

Celia's face was pale, and her red-rimmed eyes avoided meeting Janice's eyes directly. Celia's stringy, light-brown hair hung from a clumsy ponytail at the nape of her neck. The ponytail shifted as she tucked her head into her shoulders and said, "Hi, is Mrs. Mendenhall in?"

Janice didn't answer immediately. It seemed to Booker that she was solving a puzzle in her head. Celia didn't look up, even though the quiet seemed to stretch into forever.

"Did you have an appointment?" Janice asked, her voice soft, her question piercing.

"No. Did I need one?"

Mrs. Mendenhall was the guidance counselor, and she required everyone to meet with her over things like SAT testing and college applications.

Every time Booker had met with her, Mrs. Mendenhall had said, "My door is always open. No appointment necessary." The point of the counselor was to be available to counsel whenever somebody needed counseling.

"I can come back when I have an appointment, I guess. I'll make one later."

"No!" Janice actually jumped to her feet and raised her hand as if to stop Celia from leaving the office. "No," she said more calmly. "I'm sure Mrs. Mendenhall would love to talk to one of our students. Stay. I'll let her know that you're here."

Janice turned toward Mrs. Mendenhall's office. But then her

eyes flicked to Booker as though wanting to ask him to stand guard before she shook her head and turned back to Celia. "Why don't you come with me? We'll go together."

Yes, that woman knew something. How or why or even what, Booker didn't know. But what he did know from the way the secretary's eyes softened was that Janice was on Celia's side.

Celia followed Janice down the short, narrow hallway to Mrs. Mendenhall's office. Booker stayed where he was and tried to listen without looking like he was eavesdropping.

Janice knocked on the doorframe. "Hello, Mrs. Mendenhall. Celia Cameron is here to see you. I told her you wouldn't have any trouble making time for her today. I hope that's all right. It is, isn't it?"

It was a classic example of leading the witness. But Celia seemed too nervous to care about the manipulation of adults.

"Celia Cameron?" Mrs. Mendenhall sounded genuinely surprised.

Booker heard the abrupt squeak of a chair and knew Mrs. Mendenhall had stood and crossed the room. "Of course I have time. Come in, Celia. Come in."

Celia hovered at the door. Booker wondered if she would change her mind and tell the counselor to skip it. But she straightened her shoulders as if deciding that whatever she needed to say, she would say it.

Celia stepped over the threshold into Mrs. Mendenhall's office. The door closed.

Janice returned to her desk and was obviously preoccupied because she didn't look Booker's way when he crept down the hall to Mrs. Mendenhall's office.

He felt guilty and grateful at the same time. Guilty because eavesdropping was a jerk move. Grateful because he had the mail to put in the teachers' boxes, and those boxes just happened to be right next to the counselor's office. He had an excuse.

Once Celia started talking, her voice dropped too low for Booker to really hear everything, and Mrs. Mendenhall didn't do any talking, so there was no way to infer full information. But the few things he did overhear made him feel like throwing up.

Celia had been hurt. A lot.

He quietly walked back to the front of the office. He would finish with the mail later. Celia had been through enough. She didn't deserve for him to steal her privacy too.

When the door opened again, Mrs. Mendenhall instructed Celia to wait while she made some phone calls. Mrs. Mendenhall looked ghostly white as she offered him a thin smile on her way out of the office. Celia waited a moment before she joined him in the front of the office. He looked around, but Janice had also left her post at her desk.

It was Celia and Booker.

He didn't know why he expected her eyes to be bloodshot from crying, but he felt real surprise that her eyes were clear.

She stared at him, which made him feel awkward considering the silence between them, so he said the first thing that came to his mind.

"You're wearing Addison's hoodie."

She looked down and seemed to consider his statement before her head shot up again.

"You mean Addison Thoreau?"

"Yeah."

He could almost hear her thinking, *Isn't that the girl who tried to kill herself?* Instead, she said, "I didn't know it was—anyway, she loaned it to me this morning because my shirt . . . Well, she said she had a spare."

"What was wrong with yours?"

"It's a fact that getting ready in the dark has definite drawbacks."

"Why were you getting ready in the dark?" He wanted to stop talking, to stop asking questions, but she didn't retreat to Mrs. Mendenhall's office, and he had to fill the awkward silence with something.

It surprised him when she tilted her head and stared at him for a long moment before saying, "My mom doesn't always like me going to school. If I keep quiet and don't turn on any lights, I can sneak out before she wakes up."

He knew enough to not ask her anything else because clearly *anything else* was related to why she had come to the counselor's office.

"Addison's a good person." Celia's quiet voice broke into his thoughts.

He stiffened. Had he heard her right? "What?"

"Addison. She's a good person. Don't let the rumors about her convince you of anything different."

"No. I wouldn't. I know she's a good person."

Celia watched him for a moment before nodding. "Weren't you guys a thing?"

He shook his head. "No. But we were friends—*are* friends."

"Did you hear me in there—just now?"

He thought about lying, but he'd heard enough to feel like she didn't deserve to be lied to. "Not much. I moved away so you could have privacy."

Her jaw tightened, and a tiny crease appeared in her forehead as if she'd just had a headache settle right above the bridge of her nose. "Thanks for that." Celia let the silence stretch between them, then said, "This morning, I realized my shirt had holes in it, but I didn't realize it until I got to school. That YouTuber kid . . ." She shook her head. "Anyway, I hid in the bathroom because I didn't want Officer Whitfield to see me—to notice what the holes meant. Because someone noticing would be disastrous, right? I mean, wouldn't it?"

Booker jiggled his head, not quite sure if he was nodding or shaking it, and definitely not sure what she was really talking about.

"I can't believe I'm telling you this," she said.

She looked out the office's glass partitions as if checking to see if Mrs. Mendenhall or Janice might be coming back to save her from spilling secrets. They weren't coming. And she didn't stop talking.

"I've almost told a million times. Maybe a million times a million. But *almost telling* isn't the same thing as *telling*, is it? And now that I've done it, telling isn't as bad as I thought it would be. That was a fact I didn't expect."

Booker didn't even dare head-jiggle in case it reminded her that she really didn't want him to hear her confession.

"My mom's not a monster," she said abruptly, her tone changing to something manic. "I know what you think, but she's not."

Did Celia know what he thought? How could she when he wasn't sure what he thought?

"I'm just saying there's people worse off than me. I have a roof over my head, food to eat, a bed that's mine. How many people in the world can say that? And okay, I don't actually know how many people can say that, but I'm probably in the majority, first-world problems and all that."

She'd talked him into a dizzying spiral of confusion.

"I thought about the things I could do. Like running away,

but then there's the food-and-shelter thing." She sucked in a deep breath. "I even thought about going to live with my dad." She sputtered a laugh like she'd said something repulsive and hilarious all at the same time. She shook her head. "His new wife looks at me like I'm mud dripping on an expensive white carpet. I don't think my dad hates me, though. But then, he loves the woman who hates me. It's hard to forgive him for that fact. Do you think I'm crazy?"

Booker had no idea how to answer such a question, so he turned it into a question he could ask her. "Why would I think that?"

Her shoulders hunched as she shrugged. "It's just weird that I can forgive the abuse of my own mother but not the disdain of my dad's new wife. It's funny, right?"

He didn't answer.

She pressed her lips together and let her gaze drop to the floor.

No, he thought. *Not funny.*

He didn't think she was crazy either. He just thought she was simply sad, hurt, and confused.

That was when Celia started to cry, which sent Booker into a panic.

Mrs. Mendenhall and Janice were suddenly in the office with them, though he didn't remember them coming back. Mrs. Mendenhall smiled at him and then led Celia back down the hallway.

Before Celia stepped into Mrs. Mendenhall's office, she stopped and said, "Tell Addison thanks. Tell her I'm glad she's okay."

Booker let a huge breath escape him when the door was closed again.

"You, apparently, are a trustworthy soul."

He jerked his head up to see Janice watching him. Not sure how to respond to her comment, he changed the subject.

"Um, yeah, so I have this note from my mom that I've been taking to all my teachers. Since this is sort of a class for me, I need you to know as well." He handed her the note.

Her eyebrows drew in as she read, but she nodded when she'd finished and handed the note back. "I'm sorry about your cousin, and I think you're doing a good thing by showing your support."

"You might not think that when I show up tomorrow with a bald, freaky-shaped dome." He tried to laugh, but nothing really felt funny.

"Dwayne Johnson has proven that a man doesn't need hair to be handsome." She tapped a finger against the picture of the Rock taped to the side of her desk.

That made Booker smile. He wasn't sure if he liked being compared to Janice's Hollywood crush but knew she meant well. "Thanks."

"It should be me thanking you." She nodded back to the closed door. "That girl hasn't talked to anyone in her life before now, but she opened up to you. Like I said, you definitely must be a trustworthy soul to have someone like her talk to you."

He looked back at Mrs. Mendenhall's office. "Not everyone talks to me."

After all, Addison hadn't.

10

Addison's Journal
December 7, 11:58 a.m.

I have lunch next. I'm watching the last minutes of class cycle down to where I will have to deal with lunch. I hate how it feels like grade school. Where will I sit? Will anyone sit by me? Will I be able to trust the people who do choose to sit with me? Do I trust myself not to have a meltdown in front of anyone?

How long can I avoid the hard people?

Why do I have no trouble talking to people who are practically strangers?

That's not true. Talking to strangers is hard.

Just not *as* hard.

It's especially hard when it just feels like they're trying to fix you. Both sets of people: people you know and people you don't. Having them see your broken parts no matter how carefully those parts are concealed is hard.

And we tried, my mom and me. At the beginning, it was my mom who erased our previous lives. She scoured our past so perfectly clean, what else could I do but conform? It seemed like the right solution at the time, even to me.

But I've been carrying the match of memory ever since. How was I to know how easily that match would set my world on fire?

I didn't know. But I do now.

. . . .

Celia

Celia thought maybe she'd made a mistake. She had known how to handle the shifts and pivots that came her way every day. Then she spilled all her secrets and created an incomprehensible chaos.

Fact: She didn't know how to exist in this new chaos.

Did her mom know yet? Did her mom have any idea Celia had betrayed her? What would they do to her mom? Would they arrest her? Would they arrest her boyfriend?

She wanted them to arrest the boyfriend—it bothered her that she couldn't remember his name; shouldn't she be able to remember something like that?—but she didn't want them to arrest her mom.

The school nurse, a soft-spoken Black woman named Charisma, surveyed Celia's arms and asked permission to take pictures of the wounds.

Now that the words were out and couldn't be unsaid, she hated that she'd told. What were they going to do with her? She wanted to ask. She wanted a lot of things. She asked for nothing.

A light brown-skinned woman in a dove-gray pantsuit and a soft, baby-pink blouse sat in a chair next to her and smiled. She didn't wear any makeup, not even a coat of lip gloss, but she was pretty.

Celia thought of her mom with layers of various colors over

her eyes and cheeks and lips. Celia didn't think her mom could seem pretty to anyone, but she almost always had a boyfriend, though those boyfriends were usually the type Celia thought it would be better to be without.

No relationship being better than a bad one was a thought to tuck away and consider at a different time because the woman started talking, pulling Celia back to the present. "My name is Monica. I work for the Department of Children and Families for the state of Massachusetts. Mrs. Mendenhall told me you gave her permission to call me. Is that correct?"

Celia nodded and clutched her hands tightly together, twisting her fingers into a knot. Fact: She had done this. She *had* given permission. It had seemed like a good idea at the time. She trusted Mrs. Mendenhall.

But now what? What would happen to her? Where would they take her? Would it be someplace worse?

What if they called her dad?

Would they call him, and would his new wife smirk at the fact that Celia's mom had done something so bad it involved the whole state of Massachusetts? Would her dad consider this some huge failing on Celia's part?

A guy with blond hair and fair skin, who had initially entered the office with Monica, walked past the open door. He had something white and familiar in his hands.

Her shirt.

They'd pulled the shirt out of the garbage can. How many times could that thing be resurrected like a zombie in a horror film? Why had she told Mrs. Mendenhall about throwing it away? About the girl giving up her hoodie in the bathroom? About all of everything? Why couldn't she have stayed silent?

"Excuse me." Celia interrupted whatever Monica was about to say. "What's going to happen to my mom?"

Monica had the look of a woman who understood hard things and could be compassionate. "When we finish here, we'll take you to a doctor for an assessment of your wounds and to see what we can do about getting those healing faster so they don't leave scars if possible."

Celia squeezed her hands together so tightly her fingernails cut into her and her knuckles were white. "That's me, but what's going to happen to my mom?"

"While you're with the doctor, some officers will visit your mother to let her know where you are and what is happening to you. And to let her know that we know what she did to you."

"Will she be arrested?"

"Honestly, yes. There will be an investigation, and she'll have charges brought against her. But the most important thing you need to know is that everything that will happen to her comes from her choices, not your choices. Nothing in this is your fault. I need you to understand that. Do you understand that?"

Celia swallowed hard and tried to nod that she did, for a fact, understand.

But she didn't.

"Right," Monica said. "Now, let's focus on you and your needs. When you're done with the doctor, we'll take you somewhere safe for a few days while we make plans for your future."

"My future?"

Monica's eyes filled with compassion. She leaned forward, the action making Celia flinch back defensively.

"Are you scared of me?" Monica asked.

Celia hated herself for all her newfound honesty, but she nodded.

"Dang. I even wore my pink shirt today to hide my villainy."

Funny. Monica was trying to be funny. It shouldn't have worked. Celia shouldn't have thought that such a silly joke actually held any humor, but it held enough. She offered Monica a smile. It felt small and awkward, but it was all she had to give.

"You're right. It wasn't a great joke, but I've never been good at comedy. My kids on the other hand—they're hilarious."

"You have kids?"

"Yep. A two-year-old and a five-year-old. Bossy big sister to the worshipful little sister. Very busy little people. They keep me on my toes for certain. My oldest actually picked my shirt for me this morning. She said it made her smiles happy."

Celia's own smile curved up briefly until she remembered her own shirt. She asked about it.

Monica put her elbows on her knees and leaned in again. This time Celia did not flinch away. "It's evidence that will help a judge know we have a reason to keep you out of your mom's care for a while. If the judge determines you require continued protection, then we'll work to find you a place where you'll be safer."

"And my mom goes to jail?"

"Probably. But that's not a bad thing. She can get help while she's there. It's probable that they'll work toward rehabilitating her, having her go to counseling, things like that."

Celia felt like a kindergartner lost in a store, asking childish questions and wondering where her mommy was. She tucked deeper into the hoodie Addison had given her, liking that it was soft and ironed and how it felt like a barrier between her and everything else. She pulled her hands into the sleeves and, for the first time, noticed a small tear in the hoodie, down at the bottom where it was almost invisible. A hole in her shirt and a hole in this hoodie.

So much the same thing.

So entirely different.

She told Monica that her mom hadn't always been like she was now. Before the drinking, before the drugs, her mom had been like every other mom. She wanted to defend her mother, but, really, those facts just made her current situation worse. She had known her mom at a time when her mom had been someone who loved her, and then she'd turned into this person who *didn't* love her. Celia felt like a strange sort of walking contradiction, both defending and accusing her mom. But wasn't life full of contradictions?

She inspected the tear in the hoodie and wondered how it got there as Monica continued with the basic timeline of what would happen and then introduced Celia to her partner, Rob.

She felt around the frayed edges of the tear as they bundled her into a car and helped her with the seat belt because she was too distracted to remember to put it on herself.

She poked at the tear and picked at a few of the stringy threads as Monica and Rob walked her into the hospital like a pair of guards protecting an important diplomat.

She thought about how picking at the tear in the hoodie was a lot like picking at the tattered edges of her life. She had picked at the loose threads of the ropes that had kept her from crashing into the chasm of her life. She had chosen the free fall she found herself in.

Celia wished she'd been able to see Addison before she left. She wished she would have been able to say thank you for the gift—a trade-off of one shirt with holes for another. The two shirts didn't make sense and yet made all the sense in the world.

The doctor who met them in the exam room was a young-ish woman—young enough Celia wondered how someone who looked barely older than herself could be a doctor already. The doctor's short-ish dark hair was held back with a clip, but a few stray hairs framed her dark face. They didn't seem to bother her as she put out her hand and said, "My name is Dr. Iva Paixão. I hear you have some burns on your arms, and I'm here to make sure they heal." Her accent was lyrical.

Celia nodded, liking the word *heal*.

The doctor asked a lot of questions.

Fact: Celia usually felt judged when people probed and poked at her personal life. But this woman was a doctor, and her questions felt like they came from a different space.

"Do you hurt anywhere else?" That was the question that got Celia. There were other bruises, and the doctor gingerly examined each one. Celia wondered if the doctor could tell where the bruises came from. Could she recognize the shape of a toe in the bruise at Celia's hip? Could she tell the long thin bruise on her side had come from the whip of a broken slat from the blinds?

Celia had spoken her truth out loud.

People had listened. They had believed her. They had helped her. She hadn't been sure that was how it would work. She had heard stories that it hadn't worked that way for others. But those were stories. This was her reality.

At the end of the examination, Celia put on Addison's hoodie, and it felt like being understood, protected, and safe for the first time in forever.

Addison's Journal
December 7, 12:28 p.m.

Mom called me last hour. I am so glad I remembered to turn off
my ringer because having my phone go off in the middle of class
would have been the worst. She didn't leave a message, but she
texted, asking me if I was all right.

I texted back immediately so she didn't worry if I was dead or
alive. I'm pretty sure all parents worry when their kids don't respond
immediately, but my mom would leave her shift at the hospital and
drive to the school and hunt me down to verify that I have a pulse.
Her leaving work would not be a good thing. She's a nurse. She
works with newborns.

She was at work when I . . . did what I did. She was supposed
to have stayed at work later or she might not have found me in time.
I think I'm glad my mom found me, but it's taken me some time to
come to that place. Sometimes it's creepy the way my mom knows
things. That night, she said she just felt a worry. I'm not sure what "a
worry" is, exactly, but it must be pretty intense because she sped the
whole way home from the hospital. Of course, she had to go all the
way back to the hospital once she found me. I wonder if her calling
me today was because of one of her "worries."

Not that she needs to be worried. Today has been underwhelmingly fine.

At least, if you consider eyes following me everywhere I go *fine*. If you consider whispers like slushing judgments trailing my every step *fine*. But even that is not as bad as I thought it would be. I think I can live with it.

That's progress, right? Being able to say words like *I can live* is a huge step. I think the therapist would be proud of me.

The worst is Booker. He wants to talk to me, but I don't know how to talk to him. I don't know how to explain everything. When his eyes fall on me, I feel the anger and the hurt and the betrayal. I owe him an explanation. I know I do.

It's something my therapist has talked to me about on several occasions, about how I need to talk to him and explain to him and continue a relationship with him in a way that is healthy. My therapist says that will allow me to exorcise my demons and control my future. But I don't know how to do that. That's how I ended up in the hospital in the first place. Because I simply don't know how to answer the Booker question.

I heard a song once by the band Sailing Magic. It's actually one of my favorites, so to say that I heard it once is a lie because I listen to it all the time. Look at me lying to myself in this diary-journal-thing. The lyrics are

> *Like shooting stars*
> *We rend open the night*
> *Burned bright, then burned out*

It's saying we're bright and brilliant but fleeting. What if I am *just* fleeting? What if I skip the bright and brilliant part? What if I don't have that moment where I rend open the night, but, instead, I am the one ripped open?

I can't rip Booker open too. That's not fair to him.

I need to talk to him. But not today. No. Definitely not today. Maybe not tomorrow either.

Maybe never.

. . . .

Damion

Damion drove back to school with a scowl that felt permanent. What had that all been about? He really had gone into the laundromat expecting to see Avery with a knife to her throat and some big bad drug lord demanding something from her. To find her talking to her brother's girlfriend who was holding a baby?

Talk about anticlimactic.

Not that he would've had the first idea how to handle a drug lord with a knife, but he'd been willing. It told him something about himself he hadn't been sure of before. A guy always wonders.

The way Avery looked made him wonder if she had known what to expect when she'd gone in. She looked as baffled as he felt no matter what she said about the whole thing.

To add to his list of anxieties, one of his messages from the faker accounts hinted at knowing where he lived—even though he worked diligently to keep that information private. The idea that anyone would bother him at home filled him with panic. He couldn't, wouldn't, let anyone mess with his home.

After parking his car, he raced inside the school, hoping to make it to his next class on time, but as he walked through the cafeteria doors to shortcut his way to biology, he realized that "on time" was not part of the universe's plan for him that day. Second lunch was in full swing, which meant he was already at least ten minutes late.

On his way through the cafeteria, people called out to him, waving and smiling. Since he didn't usually attend second lunch, he was apparently a novelty in this space.

Damion smiled and waved back. He tapped his fist to his chest to a few people who complimented the winter camp episode. Maybe he'd been wrong to worry about the mysterious messages bagging on him for his lack of effort with Addison Thoreau.

As that thought crossed his mind, he spied Addison out of the corner of his eye. He saw her before she saw him, before she saw anyone, really. She looked entirely out of her element, and she'd managed to make herself appear small and ignorable as she stood by the condiments. She was looking over the line as if she wasn't sure she wanted to get in it or not.

He abandoned the idea of going to class. After all, he was late enough that his tardy would be counted as an absence anyway.

Curious, he watched Addison until he saw her head turn slightly. It was the movement of someone who had decided against lunch and maybe the whole cafeteria as well. She was careful to avoid looking at people, probably because she was afraid of them looking at her.

To be fair, they probably were looking at her—at least some of them anyway. Not all. Not everyone knew what she looked like, even if they'd heard her name whispered in the halls and classrooms. He hadn't known what she looked like before Avery had told him where her locker was located.

He couldn't quite say why her avoiding attention intrigued him. He never avoided being the center of any circle. But it was a big enough school for those who wanted to hide. And even those who might be looking at her now would eventually turn away to go back into their own worlds. The curiosity about her wouldn't last forever. He'd learned that the hard way as he began his video animation career. He had to keep creating newer, bigger, better things or people would forget him.

He couldn't let people forget him.

She took a step, and he jumped into action.

If he let her leave, he might miss his chance to talk with her and be seen with her. In his rush and anxiety to keep her from reaching the exit, he almost knocked her over, especially since some other guy was coming at her with the same sort of focus. They all nearly collided in a weird triangular twist of people.

"Hey, Addison." The guy who spoke was someone Damion didn't know. But the way he greeted Addison made him sound like he wanted to hang his head in shame, and he didn't meet her eye. Weird.

If the two of them hadn't basically corralled her near the condiments, she likely would have skirted past them and made her escape.

"Booker. Hi." She cast a trembling smile to Damion to acknowledge him. The way she ducked her head and visibly paled meant she wasn't thrilled about running into the other guy, and the other guy was clearly aware that she wasn't thrilled, and taking on some serious damage by her behavior.

Damion felt ridiculously sorry for the other guy—Booker, Addison had called him.

She looked cornered because she *was*, but Booker looked guilty about it, as her eyes darted around them both, searching for a way to pass him to the exit.

"Hi," Booker repeated and then closed his mouth with a clack of teeth and a tightening of lips. He looked at Damion and then scowled as if they were in competition for Addison's attention or something. That thought of competition was probably what made Booker open his mouth to speak up again. "I was wondering if you wanted to maybe eat lunch with me."

Damion almost laughed at the whole ego battle with this random human except the panic in Addison's face amplified into something that reminded him of a ticking time bomb. He almost told Booker to take a hike, except, at that moment, Luis Serrano joined them.

Damion knew Luis because the guy was the most likely candidate for valedictorian. He was the kind of guy who didn't notice anything not directly related to his grades. He certainly didn't seem to notice that the group he'd just walked into was in the middle of, well, something. He didn't seem to notice anything at the moment above his own whining, which he'd come to share with them.

"I'm going to fail Anderson's test." Luis dragged his hand down his light-brown face and stared at them like they might be able to prevent his personal tragedy.

Addison and Booker stared back. Damion was glad to see Booker's glare widen to include Luis. As for Addison? Well, Damion didn't know what she made of the whole thing.

"Fail. As in not pass. As in never get into Yale." Luis squinted and looked harder at Addison as if something about her was different and he wasn't sure what.

Luis frowned, his dark eyebrows furrowed in a knot above his nose. "You haven't been in school lately."

Booker looked like he might kick Luis or maybe even put his hand over Luis's mouth to stop him from speaking again.

Addison stiffened but didn't respond.

The entire exchange shouldn't have been fascinating, but it was.

"Have you been sick?" Luis asked.

She blinked and gave her head a small shake. "What?"

"You've not been around. I haven't seen you in class. You didn't give an oral report when we were discussing presidents. The only way Anderson would excuse anyone from that was if they were deathly sick or already dead."

Booker cringed, and now Damion wanted to cover Luis's mouth. The guy had always been socially oblivious, not that social acumen was essential for a perfect grade point average. Even so, did the guy really not know? And the haters were hating on Damion?

But Addison smiled. It was a ghost of a smile, but it was still there. "You could say I was somewhere between deathly sick and dead."

"Dude. That sucks. You're not contagious, are you? I can't afford to get anything. I've spent the last month applying for scholarships and volunteering for stuff to amp up my applications. I still have so much to do that getting sick would be bad."

"I hope I'm not contagious. That would be . . ." She glanced at Booker and held his gaze, her smile gone entirely. "Really awful. I wouldn't wish what I had on anyone."

"So did you know about Anderson's test today?" Luis ran a hand over his upper lip.

"I did. And I'm totally prepared. So"—she took a shaky breath and looked away from Booker entirely—"want to run over my notes with me during lunch? I can definitely help you. We can head to the library so there aren't distractions."

Booker exhaled slowly. She was avoiding the guy, obviously. But why? He looked harmless enough, and he seemed to care about her best interests or he wouldn't have been so uptight about Luis's less-than-tactful questions.

"I could help you guys study if you'd like." Booker's interjection sounded desperate, even to Damion. "We could do a cram session with the three of us and get you ready."

Damion felt all the awkward in the situation, which was only made worse when Addison ignored the question entirely and Luis squinted up at Damion and declared, "Hey! You're Damion Archer, the YouTube guy! Dude, you're famous!"

Damion smiled. "That's me, I guess."

"I didn't know you were friends with Booker and Addison."

"We just met," Booker said at the same time Addison said, "Yeah, we're friends."

Booker looked surprised but didn't correct Addison.

Damion felt a bit of relief. Addison had said it loud enough to be heard by anyone nearby. People were watching them now, not actively or anything but pausing sorts of glances as they passed.

Hopefully, it would get around that he'd been hanging out with Addison, that she had called him her friend. Then, even if there were rumors floating around that he was a guy just flexing his fame, people might at least question what they heard versus what they saw in reality. Maybe then the savage onslaught of messages could end. The threats to pay him a visit at home might stop.

Though they might not. He had a feeling this wasn't really about Addison but rather about people wanting to yank him back down into the mediocrity of high school. But he hoped the tide would be turning in his favor.

Addison looked down. Her eyes were at the cuff of her left sleeve as her fingers tugged it down lower over her hand.

Damion didn't know the details of Addison's issues. He'd hardly had time to find out, but he wondered if she was thinking of what happened. Did she have scars she was trying to hide? If so, what would the scars look like? Would she ever wear short-sleeved shirts again? Or would she always keep them hidden the way she did now?

He shifted uncomfortably and took a step back as Booker offered to help study again.

This time Addison responded with, "Too many people might make the studying more complicated. What do you say, Luis? You game for a little tutoring?"

"I don't want you to miss lunch." Luis looked hopeful but had given her the out, which was a decent thing to do.

She shook her head. "I don't feel like eating after all. So, no worries."

He looked conflicted. "You're really not contagious, are you?"

Damion wanted to laugh. Sure, it was a totally inappropriate thing for Luis to say, which made it even more hilarious.

As if Addison could read his thoughts, she made eye contact with Damion while saying to Luis, "No. Just not hungry."

"Then, yes. A thousand times, yes. My future career as a congressman thanks you."

"Great!" Addison sounded way more enthusiastic than a study slam deserved as she grabbed Luis by the arm and used him as a human shield to bulldoze her way past Booker and Damion.

Booker tried one more time. "But, Addison, I thought we could talk a minute."

"Sure we can," she said too fast, too brightly. "Later. You don't want Luis to fail his test and ruin his career, do you?"

Booker didn't answer but stared after them for a long time. "Future congressman needs help with US history? Weak," he grumbled before apparently remembering Damion was there, observing the whole thing. Booker looked him up and down. "YouTube, huh?"

"Yep."

"You really famous?"

Damion laughed. "Maybe not as much as I thought before today. But I do okay."

"When did you start hanging out with Addison?"

Such an honest question deserved an honest answer. "This morning. I'm on the Hope Squad."

Booker seemed relieved by that news. And the entire exchange assured Damion that at least it wasn't Booker sending him hate messages. Since Booker sent serious overprotective-boyfriend vibes, he had started to inch up on Damion's list of possible suspects.

"Want to get some lunch?" Damion asked since he still hadn't eaten.

Booker agreed, and soon they were sitting at a cafeteria table eating pizza together. "So, Booker. What's your story?"

Already, Damion knew a little about Booker: the guy folded his pizza in half, careful not to get his fingers greasy in the process. You learned a lot about people by their rituals.

"No story."

"I just watched you watch a girl you clearly have the hots for."

"Was it that obvious?" Booker stared at his folded pizza as if it was something dredged up from the bottom of a garbage can instead of an awesome lunch.

"Frosty the Snowman's carrot nose is less obvious."

"She makes me . . . argh!" He growled out the last bit.

Damion tried not to laugh at the unexpected outburst.

Sometimes seeing the humor in most everything got him into a lot of trouble.

Booker explained some of his angst regarding Addison and then moved on to his cousin who had cancer.

Damion ate two full slices before Booker even took a bite of his own folded-up pizza. The guy clearly had a lot going on. Damion couldn't figure out why Booker chose to talk to him. They didn't even know each other. Maybe it was because he'd said he was on the Hope Squad.

Booker then mentioned shaving his hair off that night with his cousin. "Do you want to come?"

Damion wasn't exactly sure what Booker was getting at but didn't need to ask for clarification because Booker quickly added, "To the head-shaving party. It's tonight at my house. My mom's making food, which means there will be lots of things to eat and . . ." He paused as a group of girls stopped by to flirt and say hello to Damion.

Damion did what he could to make each girl feel listened to. After spending time with Addison, he wondered how many people at his school needed to be listened to for a minute. Booker proved that probably everyone needed someone to just listen once in a while.

"So you really are famous," Booker said after another person had stopped by to talk about the winter camp episode.

Damion shrugged.

Booker shook his head. "Never mind about the head-shaving party. You wouldn't be interested in that."

"Whoa! You can't uninvite me after inviting me. That's just not cool. Text me your address and the time, and I'll come if I can. If I can't, I'll let you know. I have some pretty intense personal stuff going on right now, so don't panic if I can't." Damion paused, wondering if he should tell Booker about his own personal mayhem, but the guy seemed to have a lot on his shoulders already. Did he need Damion's troubles too? No. No one needed that. Besides, Damion was the Hope Squad guy, not Booker.

Another group came over to say hello.

"Must be nice to be famous," Booker said.

"It has its moments," Damion said. His phone chimed with an incoming direct message. He didn't want to look. He shouldn't have looked, but he'd blocked several accounts already, so maybe this was something good? He couldn't keep himself from glancing at the screen and seeing the words:

2 late to act like u care about Addison now FAKER! People will see u for the faker you've always been.

He blinked, his head shooting up to scan the crowded cafeteria. Whoever was sending the messages was in the room with him, had seen him with Addison. Yet, being seen with her didn't do the good he had hoped.

"Having everyone know who you are . . ." Booker clucked his tongue. "That's gotta be cool."

Damion's jaw tightened, and he blinked the burn from his eyelids. "Not everyone who knows me likes me." He frowned and felt the deeper pain—that pain he never showed anyone at all—push to the surface of his emotions. "And worse, not even everyone knows me."

Addison's Journal
December 7, 12:42 p.m.

Damion talked to me again. Like, went out of his way to talk to me. He says no one put him up to it, but . . . why? I want to ask him why he's talking to me, but I don't want to come off rude. Would it be rude? I am so done hurting people. Like hurting Booker. Booker is furious with me. I felt the back of my head burning up with his glare as I walked away with Luis. I should have let Booker come too. It's not like I would've been alone with him. It was the best possible scenario—letting him spend time with me like things were fine while having the buffer of another human to keep us safe.

Safe. I don't know why I said it that way. I'm so messed up.

Luis wasn't lying when he said he was going to fail Anderson's exam. I had to stop myself from asking him where he's been all se-mester. But I'm betting he has his own drama in his personal life. Don't we all?

I've resorted to the cheat of mnemonics. It's easier to know a thing forever if someone teaches you a trick to learn it. I hate how many things the word *mnemonics* dredges up for me. It's good Booker didn't come to the library with us. Not after the last time we were in the library together, where I'd glimpsed into one of my hells through a door I'd thought I'd bolted and padlocked shut.

Booker opened the door just a crack, but it was enough to force me to battle a demon only I could see. If he was here, now, would that cracked-open door open wider? Didn't it open wider anyway as I fake-smiled and helped Luis create a mnemonics list for the facts we need to memorize for the test?

I can hear him whisper the word MAIN as his pencil scratches over his paper because he says if he writes it down, it will help him remember. The four main causes of World War I: Militarism, Alliance system, Imperialism, Nationalism. I recite along with him as he whisper-writes. All I can do is wish I could shake the memory of why I understand why mnemonics work out of my head. But I don't do that. I'm writing here instead. I wonder if writing it down is making me fracture even more.

· ·

Avery

There's a baby in my brother's room. My brother's baby is in my brother's room. My nephew is in my brother's room.

The words marched through Avery's head like a parade on an endless loop.

Holy bananas.

She'd walked down the hall after leaving Jo and little baby Tyler to get settled, but then she went back and knocked on the door.

"Come in!" Jo's voice called out.

She twisted the knob, opened the door, and leaned onto the doorframe. "I'm gonna have to tell my dad."

Jo's eyes widened so slightly that if Avery hadn't been looking for signs of distress, she would have missed it altogether.

Jo stood from where she'd been creating a makeshift bed for the baby in the corner of the room. "I can leave. I don't want to be a bother."

"Calm down. I'm not asking you to leave. First, there is no way to hide a baby in this house. Second, there is no way I'm not telling my dad he has a grandson. I think my brother is a jackbag for not saying anything to us sooner, and I don't want to make that same mistake. And I'm not going to lie and say my dad is going to be totally cool with this. I don't honestly know what his reaction will be, but my dad's not a monster. He's actually a really good guy. He won't kick you out. He was softer when my mom was alive, but that was a long time ago. Maybe a baby will soften him up again, maybe not, but it'll be easier on all of us if we start with the truth and go from there."

"I don't have anywhere else to go," Jo said.

"I know. And you're not going anywhere else. But my dad isn't an idiot. He'll figure it out, and then he might actually make you go because we weren't honest in the beginning. See? That's how my dad works. When we were kids and did something wrong, we'd be in trouble for the wrong thing we did. But lying about the thing we did wrong was the unforgivable sin."

She thought about how much tension existed between her dad and brother and how the root of all that tension was the fact that Tyler lied all the time. Lied about where he was. Lied about who he was with. Lied about what he was doing.

Her dad would be mad about the fact that he'd withheld the whole kid information, too, but he couldn't possibly hold that against Jo and the baby.

At least Avery didn't think he would.

"I'll make us some lunch. Come down when you're ready." Avery left, closing the door behind her.

She ended up making peanut butter and jelly sandwiches. Basic? Yes. But also universally acceptable when it came to picky eaters. Maybe Jo wasn't a picky eater, but Avery didn't want to take chances. She only hoped Jo didn't have peanut allergies.

While waiting for Jo to come down, she flipped open the Chromebook she'd bought for a great deal on eBay and went to YouTube. When she found herself on Damion's channel, she almost closed her Chromebook again. What was she thinking, going to his stupid channel?

She didn't close the Chromebook. She clicked play on the most recent video.

About halfway through the episode, a laugh from behind her startled her.

"That's funny!" Jo said.

Avery hit pause and glanced around. "Where's . . ."

"Tyler's napping. He always naps after he gets fed."

Avery glanced at the sandwiches on plates. She'd pulled out milk for the baby but then put it back because she hadn't been sure if he could do regular milk or if he needed formula. "Fed?"

"Yeah. Breastfeeding is way cheaper than formula. The lactation nurse taught me that at the hospital. Well, she taught breastfeeding was healthier anyway. But it helps that it's so much cheaper too."

Avery turned away, feeling her face grow warm and not sure why. Jo had just referenced something perfectly natural and normal. Avery disguised her embarrassment by pulling the two plates with sandwiches from the counter and taking them over to the table where they could sit and eat.

Jo followed her, sat down, and picked up her sandwich. "Thanks for this. I'm really hungry."

Avery wondered when the last time the girl had eaten and

then chided herself for thinking of Jo as a girl. She was older than Avery by two years. And she was a mom besides. But it didn't stop Avery from feeling like the grown-up between the two of them.

"So the voice on that cartoon you were watching—he sounded like the guy who drove us here."

"Yeah. It's one and the same." Avery frowned at her sandwich and took a bite that felt more like snapping her jaws over Damion's head. Though it wasn't fair for her to be angry with him when he'd been nothing but nice. Just because she was uncomfortable with her reality and just because rich, fancy, popular, jackbag Damion had witnessed her reality didn't make her reality his fault. *What must he think of me?*

"He seems nice. Not like any of the guys in my neighborhood."

"He's not really like any of the guys in my neighborhood either."

Technically, Damion lived only a few streets away from her. But the houses where he lived were these sprawling things with too much room and cars parked in garages instead of on the street. What a difference a few streets made.

They ate their sandwiches in silence. Jo finished hers much faster and bit her lip as she looked around the small kitchen. She'd said she was hungry. What if one sandwich wasn't enough?

"Would you like another one?" Avery finally asked.

"Yes. Please." Jo answered so quickly Avery felt like a monster for not making her two from the start.

Avery abandoned her own food, pushing back her chair.

Jo stood up quickly. "I can do that. You don't have to make it for me."

Avery nodded, then moved her own lunch back to the counter to nibble at while she watched Jo make another sandwich.

"Where did you meet my brother?" she asked.

"At a party. He was super chill, just all no drama—so different from the other guys who didn't know how to take no for an answer, ya know?"

Avery didn't know. She didn't date much. She never had time. She was too busy working at Meal Minute Drive-Through, which was nothing more than a shack in a parking lot where she made corn dogs and mixed sodas. She also took tutoring jobs on the side. Usually ones involving math.

If school and work weren't enough, she was also busy mothering her older brother. He always seemed to find himself on the wrong end of the right thing to do. Their dad was always mad. And Avery was always exhausted. She felt like she had to keep an eye on Tyler, keep him out of trouble. But whenever she turned around, he'd done some new stupid thing.

She opened her mouth to vent her frustrations, then looked at Jo and stuffed her sandwich in her mouth instead. Jo didn't need to hear Avery's worries. She had her own.

"You dating anyone?" Jo asked as she finished screwing the lid onto the peanut butter. She leaned against the counter, making no move to head back to the table, and licked up the side of her sandwich so the grape jelly wouldn't fall out.

"No," Avery said, finishing up her own meal and rinsing her hands in the sink. "Not really looking for that kind of thing right now."

"That's too bad. I think the guy who drove us today likes you."

Avery barked out a laugh. "Damion? No. You read that

totally wrong. Damion owed me a favor. That's why he was playing chauffeur today."

She shrugged her too-skinny shoulders. "That's not what I saw."

"Right. And what did you see?"

"Him thinking you needed to be rescued. He rushed into that laundromat like he was ready to save you even though he seemed a little scared."

"He probably was scared. He thinks that because my brother deals drugs, I do too. He's famous, and I'm nobody."

"He didn't look at you like you were nobody. When you were looking out the car window, he kept looking at you."

How did this conversation even get started? "Look, we were friends when we were in grade school, but that was, like, dinosaur-ages long ago."

"Tyler said you were like this."

Avery blinked. "Like what?"

Jo shrugged. "Closed off. He said when your mom died, you shut down."

Avery scoffed. "Oh, because Tyler knows anything." She shoved away from the counter and retrieved both plates to rinse and put in the dishwasher. "Tyler went death-wish reckless after Mom died."

Jo shrugged again. "He said that too. He said it was because he was so sad. He said you were so sad, too, but wouldn't talk about it. It sounds like you were both dealing with depression. I'd say you both still are."

"Depression? How is being responsible depression? One of us had to stay functional and grounded and realistic or Dad wouldn't have any family left."

"Sorry. I wasn't trying to . . . sorry. Can I help with anything? I want to earn the space you're giving me."

Avery sighed. She hadn't meant to snap at Jo. "No. There really isn't anything to do right now. You should get some rest and make Tyler's room your own space as much as you can. When my dad comes home, we'll tell him everything."

Jo nodded, her mouth turned downward. She walked toward the kitchen entrance to the stairs.

Avery rolled her eyes at herself for basically dismissing this woman. "Hey, Jo?"

Jo turned to look at Avery. "Yeah?"

"I'm glad you're here. I'm glad I have this chance to be with you and my nephew."

"Thanks. I'm glad too. And, yeah, it's probably not my place to say anything, but I really do think that cartoon guy likes you. Like, totally into you."

Avery didn't argue. She just laughed. "I appreciate your belief in such a possibility. We were friends a long time ago, but not now."

Jo shrugged—a thing that seemed to be her default reaction. Then she was gone, leaving Avery standing in her kitchen and thinking about everything Jo said regarding Damion.

When Avery had told Addison Thoreau that maybe she and Damion would be friends someday, *maybe*, Addison had said something about how, in the future, Avery might wish she'd started being Damion's friend today or something like that.

Avery frowned. Maybe they were right?

Maybe.

And all that stuff about her and Tyler dealing with depression? As defensive as she might've felt over it, she knew it was true. Tyler had used drugs to self-medicate his depression. Avery had crawled into her own head and used her schoolwork as her escape. If she made herself too busy to feel it, then it didn't exist.

But she knew that wasn't true. She'd learned in her psychology class that strong, healthy relationships helped those who suffered from depression to cope. If she had tried to be one of those strong relationships for her brother, would he have landed himself in jail? If she allowed healthy relationships in her own life, would she be better able to cope?

She put the jelly back in the fridge, paced the kitchen a few times, which didn't take long since the kitchen wasn't exactly big, and pulled her phone from her pocket.

She sent a text to Damion.

∴ ✳ 13 ✳ ∴

Addison's Journal
December 7, 1:14 p.m.

I finished my test before the majority of the class, and so I've got some time to do what I want until class is over. I hope Luis does well. I can practically hear his brain reciting mnemonics from here.

Okay. Fine. Here's why I know how to use mnemonics. My stepdad taught me.

My stepdad.

When was the last time those two words ever took up occupancy in my brain?

It is sad that I know the answer to that. It had been December then too. It had been cold then too. But I hadn't been seventeen. I'd been nine.

The last time he'd hurt me had not been the first time. It had just been the time I was old enough to be done with all of it. My mom was leaving town for the weekend to take some continuing-education classes as a nurse. My stepdad was in charge of baby-sitting me while she was gone. I kissed her goodbye and packed a grocery bag with my blanket and favorite stuffed owl. I liked him best because he had big eyes. It made me believe he would watch over me while I slept. But by then I knew he didn't, or if he did, he didn't do anything to help me. But I still loved him best even though I was nine and too old for stuffed animals.

I had a dollar fifty-eight in change so I could buy food. That's funny to think about now. What was I really going to buy for a dollar fifty-eight?

I slipped out my window while he said goodbye to Mom. I climbed down the trellis, and I didn't even fall when my jacket got caught on a nail.

I went to a park where Mom always took me but where he never had gone with us. In my mind, that meant he didn't know where the park was and wouldn't find me. Wouldn't hurt me again.

It's strange to remember so clearly the things I have felt forbidden to think for so long. The therapist says trauma plants itself like a cancerous growth. She says it stays hidden for as long as it can, getting bigger and bigger and consuming more and more of the good cells. We only ever find cancer because a sudden pain tells us it's there.

Mom found me the next morning. She'd come home from class early because my stepdad called the police when he'd found me missing. The police called my mom.

I don't remember her finding me. I only know she did because I woke up in a hospital. It had been so cold with only my blanket and my owl for warmth. I remember curling up next to a light embedded in the sidewalk. I thought its glow would give heat. I don't remember much else.

I had hypothermia. But I didn't die. He probably wished I had because that's when I told on him. I was in a hospital, surrounded by other adults. I felt protected. I felt brave.

Mom believed me. She started punching him. The doctors had to pull her off him. We never went back to that house. She took us away, put him in prison, and told me I was never, ever to talk about it again because that man did not deserve our words. She told me I was never to think of it again because that man did not deserve our thoughts.

So I didn't.

Not once.

Not until the therapist. Telling her was one thing, but now I'm writing all this down where anyone can find it. Where anyone can see. What am I thinking? I'm going to have to tear this page out of this book and burn it as soon as I get the chance.

I should call my mom. I should go home.

Why did I write any of this?

I've got to get out of here!

• •

Booker

Booker left the cafeteria before lunch was actually over. Damion had received a few messages or something and said he had to take care of some stuff, so he didn't feel like a jerk for abandoning the guy. Not that he would have been on his own. Booker was pretty sure they hadn't passed a single two-minute span without someone stopping to knuckle-bump or high-five Damion. The guy had a solid fan base. It was both awesome and bizarre to watch unfold in a high school cafeteria.

He didn't go to the library because he didn't trust himself to not demand Addison talk to him even with Luis there to witness the whole conversation. He could wait. He could be patient. She couldn't avoid him forever.

Except he worried that she could. She'd been doing a pretty good job of it so far.

She obviously doesn't want to talk to you, so forget her and move on with your life, he told himself over and over. It was like an anti-pep talk. His internal rants were in direct contradiction to the positivity poster tacked on the painted cinder-block wall outside Mr. Anderson's classroom door.

This year's positivity poster was slightly smaller than last year's, if the blue smudges from the leftover adhesive were any indicator. He hadn't paid much attention to the previous poster because he'd always shared his lunch hour with Addison, and they always seemed to get to class just before the bell rang. Who had time to look at positive messages when detention was on the line?

But now he inspected the new poster as thoroughly as if it might be part of Mr. Anderson's test. It was an image of a guy and a girl free-climbing a mountain framed in black. Within the black framing was a quote by Dale Carnegie in white bolded letters. The font was sans serif—the kind of font that wanted to be clear in its message, without any little scrolls or loops to get in the way.

"Most of the important things in the world have been accomplished by people who have kept on trying when there seemed to be no hope at all."

He wondered if Addison had ever read the poster before. If she had, would it have made a difference in her decision to stop trying? Would her attempt have never happened? Would she still be reachable as his friend?

Because he would have been happy with just that—her friendship—even if it meant they never actually dated or got closer. Even though he really wanted to see what happened if their relationship became something more, he wanted her friendship most of all.

They'd been friends for years. How could it all be so different now?

He waited for Addison and Luis to return from the library, his mood falling with each student that showed up who wasn't them.

A few kids cast him curious looks from their desks, where they watched him stubbornly stand guard in the hall, but he ignored them. He wasn't the kind of guy who cared what other people thought—not really.

Except he cared what Addison thought. That was why he felt so desperate to talk to her. He cared what she thought a whole lot.

He also cared what Mr. Anderson thought, but his teacher was engrossed in a book on his desk. His hands were in his reddish-brown hair, which was pretty thick considering Mr. Anderson was probably in his fifties. There were thirty-six seconds before the bell went off. Mr. Anderson counted not being in your seat as a tardy. If Booker got another one, it would count as an absence. He called it. They weren't coming—at least not in time for the bell.

Maybe she convinced Luis to scrap the test and ditch class altogether. But why would she want Luis for that sort of thing and not Booker?

Booker slid into his seat as Addison and Luis raced through the door.

Mr. Anderson finger-combed his hair, probably realizing he'd been messing it up while he'd been reading, and looked up from his desk to see who the tardy interlopers were but stopped upon seeing Addison. Instead of calling out, "That's a tardy, Mr. Serrano and Miss Thoreau," like he always did when someone was late, he hesitated, then looked away as they slid into their seats. He smiled to welcome the rest of the class.

Part of Booker felt grateful Mr. Anderson hadn't called them out. He didn't want to see Addison hurt or embarrassed. The other part of him that liked the world to be fair for everyone scowled. Equality was a conundrum sometimes. Nowhere was that clearer to Booker than in US history.

Luis shifted in his seat behind Booker. He put his hands on Booker's shoulders and leaned in to whisper, "Your girlfriend saved me, man. I think I'll actually pass this test." A fist showed up in Booker's peripheral. Serrano was waiting for a knuckle-bump.

Booker twitched at the happiness the word *girlfriend* gave him, but he shrugged it off and touched his knuckles to Luis's. It was hard to be mad at a guy who was so sincere. And it was hard to be jealous when Serrano had called Addison Booker's girlfriend.

It wasn't true, of course, but he liked the sound of it. And it made him hope that she'd maybe said something while they were studying—something nice about him or whatever.

Booker was grateful he sat toward the back of class. It meant he didn't have to worry about Addison sitting behind him and staring at him and possibly even glaring at him.

But why would she glare? Booker shook his head and tried to focus on Mr. Anderson's test instructions.

Mr. Anderson had a passion for history. He paced the front of the room like he was the ringmaster of his own circus. Booker normally liked Mr. Anderson's antics. But today . . . today he was just annoyed by them.

Mr. Anderson finished his instructions. Tests were passed down the row, and everyone hunched over the papers on their desks and began scratching pencils.

Everyone except Booker.

He watched Addison, the way her long, dark hair fell out of

the sloppy bun she favored as a hairstyle, the way she focused on the papers in front of her, the way she tapped her pencil lightly on her desk as she read the question. He watched until he felt like a stalker. This was the second class he'd spent staring at her, and he had a test to take as well. He blinked and looked up to see Mr. Anderson watching him with an eyebrow raised.

Great. The teacher had caught him staring and likely also thought he was a stalker. Booker nodded at Mr. Anderson, who nodded back. Booker dove into the test.

After class, Serrano called for Addison to hang back in a way Booker wanted to but hadn't dared, not with the way she'd ignored, avoided, and fled from him all day.

Addison glanced at the door with a longing that made Booker frown, but she hung back anyway.

"I totally aced that!" Luis said.

"That's great." Addison glanced at the door again, bouncing a little on the balls of her feet as if preparing to run.

"You're a brave person to take on the challenge of teaching me," Serrano said, talking to her easily, like nothing was wrong, like Addison's attempt wasn't there, hanging over all of them. Of course, Serrano didn't know about the attempt. He was a studious guy who didn't have time for gossip. So he might never know. Booker envied him that ignorance.

Addison smiled a little at being called brave. "Well, my mom did say this morning that I was braver than I believed."

Serrano snorted out a laugh. "Wow. Parents, right? Nothing says I love you like Winnie the Pooh platitudes."

Addison laughed, the sound thin and forced. "She said I was stronger than I seem too. All the way Winnie the Pooh. When I asked her if that meant I didn't seem very strong, she said I was Leaning Tower of Pisa strong."

"Dude, she compared you to a building known for an accidental tilt?" Serrano was full-on laughing.

Booker watched as a silent witness, fascinated by Luis's ease in talking to Addison and wondering how he could join in and make it seem easy as well.

Addison shrugged. "The Pisa reference was actually pretty nice. It wasn't about whether the tilt was accidental or on purpose. It was about a building that has been leaning for, I don't know, centuries maybe. Nothing can hold itself like that without getting some pretty ripped abs."

"So she's paying you the ultimate compliment."

Addison nodded. "My mom's unconventional, but she's pretty great."

Booker opened his mouth to agree that her mom was, in fact, really great, but his intake of air made Addison look up at him.

She blinked and flushed a light red. Luis trotted back to his desk to finish gathering his things, and Addison looked like she was ready to bolt if he didn't do something to stop her.

"I was wondering if you want to come to my house tonight." Booker blurted the words before he could talk himself out of it.

"To your house? For what?"

"I'm shaving my hair off with my cousin tonight. Remember Seb? You've met him. He starts chemo tomorrow. He has cancer."

Her forehead creased slightly as if trying to remember Seb.

"I'm sorry, Booker, I don't think I—" She hitched up the strap of her backpack. "I gotta go. I'm going to be late for my next class."

"I can walk you there," Booker hurried to say.

"Why?"

The question startled him. When he didn't have an immediate answer, she hitched up her backpack again and left without another word or glance.

Luis stepped next to Booker and nodded his chin in the direction Addison had fled. "I couldn't get any of those dates to stick in my head, but she helped me figure out some easy ways to remember them. I'm willing to bet I'll never forget them. I had to ace this test to have any chance at being valedictorian this year and get the scholarships I need. Addison saved me. No doubt about it. I'd pay her back with a movie or dinner or something, but who has time for a social life?"

Booker rolled his shoulders at the twinge of jealousy he felt as he pictured Luis taking Addison to dinner. "No time for you, right? Not if you want to be valedictorian, buddy." It was a jerk move to use the guy's hope against him so he wouldn't take going on a date with Addison too seriously. But Booker didn't let himself feel guilty about it for too long because Luis bobbed his head in agreement and seemed happy to have been let off the hook of having to socialize in even the smallest way outside of school.

"I gotta get to class. Catch you later, man."

"Right. Later." But Booker didn't move. Addison's answer still rang hard and heavy in his ears. *Why?*

Why was he trying so hard when she clearly wanted nothing to do with him?

Why?

That was the question he needed answered as well.

14

Addison's Journal
December 7, 2:12 p.m.

Booker is torturing me. Why would he put me on the spot like that? Like somehow he owns all the real estate on pain street. I'm in the stupid bathroom again. I almost texted Mom to come get me, but she needs to work. She's taken off so much time already.

I also ripped out that last page in the journal. I threw it in the trash, but then I panicked and dug it out again, smoothed it out, and put it back in its place. I definitely do not want to hang on to it, but I don't want to leave it where someone might find it. I mean, the chances of someone digging something out of the trash is close to none, but just in case.

What would the therapist think of that? What would she say if she knew all my insane behavior today?

I hate Booker for making me feel like this.

Not true.

I don't hate Booker.

I'm mad at him.

Not true.

I don't know what's true.

His cousin is a nice guy. Booker and Seb are like brothers.

They'd have to be for Booker to be willing to shave off his hair. That's a big deal. Sounds like they want to turn it into a party instead of something sad and lost. Booker's wrong to invite me. A party like that is no place for someone like me. They want to celebrate the life his cousin is fighting for. The life I didn't—won't—fight for.

• •

Celia

Monica and Rob guided Celia out of the hospital where the doctor had cataloged all her bruises and welts and burns like a museum curator studying artifacts from a civilization that didn't make sense. Celia had told them about the blind-slat whip, about the kicking, the hitting, the burning. In for a penny, in for a pound. That was what her mom used to say when she was drinking too much and intended to drink more.

Celia figured she might as well tell it all. The telling and the cataloging took a lot longer than it probably should have because it seemed the words took a long time to fight past her lips.

As she got into the caseworker's car, she leaned her head back against the gray fabric and closed her eyes. Fatigue settled over her. She didn't even have the strength to lift her head when Monica tried to engage her in conversation. Was she awake enough to have understood Monica's question?

She tried to think of what might have been asked.

No.

She wasn't awake enough, and she was grateful Monica didn't address her again. Celia allowed the fatigue to immerse her into its depths. It meant she didn't have to think about what was happening to her mom or if her dad had been notified.

The car ride didn't last nearly long enough. She was still

drifting on the edge of sleep when the tires of the vehicle crunched over rocks or gravel or something that suggested they weren't driving on paved roads any longer. She forced her eyes open, surprised at how such a small act could be so hard.

They were on a long driveway leading to a white wood, two-story home that seemed enormous to Celia.

"Where are we?" Did her voice just slur like her mom's did when she'd been drinking? She swallowed hard and forced herself to speak clearly as she asked again.

"This is a safe place for you to stay until we contact your father and find a more permanent solution for you."

Celia nodded. At least she thought she was nodding.

Monica parked the car, and she and Rob got out. Rob opened Celia's door.

Fact: Getting out of that car was almost as hard as it had been to go into Mrs. Mendenhall's office.

Her legs wobbled like they'd turned into Silly String. But she managed to follow the caseworkers up the front steps to the porch. As Monica rang the doorbell, Celia moved behind her. She knew for a fact that trying to hide was childish and stupid, but knowing something and being able to do anything about it were not always the same thing.

Monica was on to her, though, and stepped to the side as a middle-aged Black woman with high cheekbones answered the door.

The woman's thin red lips curved into a smile. "Hello! Welcome! We're so glad to have you stay with us."

Celia almost smiled. The melodic sounds of the woman's voice reminded Celia of the copper wind chimes hanging from her neighbor's front porch. There was a sense of peace in that.

"My name is Sophie. My husband, Elijah, is at work right now, but he's excited to meet you, Celia."

Celia nodded, glad Sophie already knew her name so she didn't have to introduce herself. She wondered if Sophie would ask her questions about what happened, but she didn't. Instead, she ushered Celia and the caseworkers into her home.

Sophie greeted Monica and Rob like they were old friends. Celia wondered how many other kids had ended up in Sophie's care. Had any of those kids been like her? Where were those kids now? She wished she could talk to someone who had already been through what she was going through. Someone who could tell her how it was all going to end.

"Are you hungry?" Sophie asked.

Fact: Celia was starving. But she didn't want to be inconvenient.

"I'm starving," Rob said.

"Me too." Monica put her hand on her stomach as if to prove the point.

Sophie led them to her kitchen, where she cut up some fruit and vegetables. She had a small pile of string cheeses in the middle of the counter as well.

Celia took a string cheese and nibbled at it while the adults talked about mundane things like the weather and sports and classes that were available now that hadn't been available when any of them had been in high school. They included Celia in the conversation, even though all Celia did was nod or shake her head in response.

She ate a second string cheese. And then a third. She ate the apple slices and the carrot sticks. The adults ate, too, but she was pretty sure they only did so that she would.

She was glad because she was really hungry.

And tired.

As if sensing her exhaustion, Monica said it was time for them to go, and Rob agreed. Sophie and Celia went with them to the door.

"Sophie will take you to school tomorrow morning, and we'll come by to check on you in the afternoon, okay?" Monica said.

Celia nodded, glad they said she was going to school. She hadn't been sure even though they'd mentioned it while she'd been eating snacks like a five-year-old kid.

She couldn't seem to make herself take care of herself. Which was stupid because she'd been taking care of herself for years. She'd been taking care of her mom, too, making sure her mom got dinner and that the house chores were done.

How had she gone from handling everything to being incapable of handling anything at all?

"Don't worry," Rob said. "You're safe."

They said goodbye, and then Monica and Rob were gone, leaving Celia alone with Sophie.

"Would you like to see your room?" Sophie asked.

Celia nodded again. She tightened her lips together, glad she could communicate without speaking.

Sophie took her up the stairs, down a hall, and opened the third door on the right. She let Celia enter first. The pale-yellow room was small, with a dormer window that faced the front yard. Tucked under the low roofline was a twin-sized bed covered in a white bedspread. Sophie had to be a very brave woman to take in kids from who knew where and let them sleep in a bed with a white comforter. Celia didn't think there was anything white in her entire household aside from the burned shirt that had been pulled from the garbage and taken as evidence against her mom.

Sophie smiled. "This is all yours while you're with us. The bathroom is across the hall where you can get ready for bed tonight—you know, brush your teeth, wash your face, and all that. No one else will use it except you while you're with us, so don't worry about taking too long in the shower or anything."

Celia shifted uncomfortably. She didn't have any clothes to change into so what would be the point of a shower? She didn't have so much as a toothbrush.

Sophie took a long look at Celia, then opened the top drawer of a dresser and rummaged through it. Was she going to remove any valuables? Did she think Celia was a thief? Celia was about to run down the stairs and chase the caseworkers down the street to tell them she didn't think this was going to work. The last thing she wanted was to be treated like she was when staying with her dad and his wife.

Sophie pulled out a pair of black lounge pants. "You look like even a small might drown you, but I don't have any extra-small anymore. I hope these will work. I'll need to go shopping sometime soon." She also handed her a white T-shirt. "These are yours to keep if you'd like. There are new socks in the bottom drawer, and a new toothbrush and other toiletries are in the bathroom cupboard next to the towels."

Sophie didn't wait for Celia to say thank you or to acknowledge the kindness shown. She just smiled and said, "Get settled, take some time if you need, or come hang out with me. We eat dinner at six, when Elijah gets home. If you want, you can come down to help make dinner. I would love the company."

Help make dinner?

With someone?

Had she ever made dinner *with* someone instead of just *for* someone?

Someone who wanted her company?

Each thought felt foreign and unreal. Celia opened her mouth to speak, but Sophie was already gone.

She ran her hand over the clothes she'd received. It was the second time clothing had been offered to her that day. And both offerings had felt like a hand pulling her out of the dark and closer to light—closer to normal. She set the clothes on the bed, grateful she'd have something comfortable to sleep in.

She peeked into the hall to make sure Sophie had really gone, and then she inched the bottom drawer open. It was stuffed full with different kinds of socks. Ankle socks, no-show socks, long socks that went to the knee. They were as varied in color as they were in size. And many of them had fun and quirky designs. She picked up a pair and felt the thickness and weight of them. These weren't the cheap, thin things she always wore. These were socks of substance.

She opened the other bottom drawer and found under-clothes. Maybe Sophie hadn't mentioned it because she was embarrassed. No. That didn't feel right. It was more likely she hadn't wanted to embarrass Celia.

Who was this woman who was willing to take in total strangers at a moment's notice and give them gifts and make them feel welcomed?

As far as Celia knew, her mother had never given anything to a stranger.

Fact: Her mother barely gave anything to *her*.

Celia frowned, the guilt of comparing her mother to Sophie feeling like a hot fire over her nerves. Just because her mother had never given her socks like the ones in the drawer didn't mean her mom didn't love her.

Humming came from somewhere in the house. Sophie must have already started making dinner.

Celia pushed up her left sleeve to reveal a few of the burns that had been treated at the hospital. Didn't those burns mean her mother *didn't* love her?

She didn't know. She had her suspicions but didn't want to look too closely at the problem.

She had a hard time processing the hot and cold contrast between where she'd woken up versus where she would sleep. She imagined what things would be like when she was an adult. What sort of household would she wake up in and fall asleep in? Could she choose something more than she knew? Did she have the right to expect more out of life than what she'd been given so far? The thought made her body feel heavy and impossible to move.

But hadn't she lived through a dozen or more impossibilities that day?

She forced herself to her feet; the motion that should have been easy and quick took several minutes to accomplish.

She went downstairs to help Sophie in the kitchen.

·∴·∗**15**∗·∴·

Addison's Journal
December 7, 2:53 p.m.

A lot of people lie about who they are and where they've been. They come to the internet to reinvent themselves. For a long time, I wasn't allowed on the internet. My mom worried about the world having access to my private thoughts. She didn't need to worry.

I lie online. I think most people do.

I never talk about the things I worry about or fear. I never mention the depression that sits heavy in my stomach. There is no need to trouble the world with my troubles. So my Instagram is filled with pictures of butterflies and trees and sunsets. I don't do TikTok because the idea of making a video feels too intensely personal.

One of the last things I posted on Instagram was a selfie I took of Booker and me when we cut class to go to Tucker Falls. After I did what I did, I wanted to delete that picture. The happiness it shows is a lie. My closeness to another person is a lie.

I am someone else online than who I am in my head. I am someone else in person than who I am in my head.

Is everybody like that?

Or am I the only broken one?

Damion

"Thank you, Damion."

That had been the text he'd received from Avery. He didn't know why it choked him up to see those words, but it did. He'd felt pretty flayed throughout the day with the weird messages that had started as direct messages but which were now bleeding into his public feeds. He had tried to run damage control, but to no avail. The haters were determined to hate out loud. That seemed to be their thing. Haters were a viciously public yet cowardly anonymous group.

It didn't help that his chronic tardiness for the day earned him detention, which meant the time he'd carved out to work on a new video that afternoon had been trashed. Did the school really think detention resolved anything? How did making people waste time, including the poor teacher who got stuck babysitting, actually solve anything? Detention was proof of systemic illogicality.

"Put your phone away, Mr. Archer." Mr. Harris, a ruddy, middle-aged, phys-ed teacher, gave Damion the death stare until Damion tucked the device into his front pocket.

Damion wished he'd had time to message Avery back. It was strange that at the beginning of the day, Avery was the last person he'd imagined thinking about, but now? A few hours had changed a lot for him.

"Hey, Archer, I love your new video." The comment came from his right.

He turned to look at the grin beneath a flash of red hair. "Hey, Melbrook. What are you in for?"

Flynn Melbrook puffed out his cheeks in a long exhale.

"Mrs. Weber doesn't allow opposing viewpoints in her classroom."

"You mean she doesn't allow disrespect in her classroom."

Melbrook shrugged. "A lawyer might say that one man's disrespect is another man's right to a rebuttal."

"Right. Nothing like taking the perspective of contemplative commentary."

"Exactly. So, my friend, I've got some great ideas if you're ever looking for new material for your videos."

Melbrook was always working the angles. He called Damion his "friend" all the time, but Damion wasn't sure what that word meant anymore.

He couldn't remember the last time he felt like he'd had a true friend—a person looking out for him and being with him, no strings attached. Sure, he had fans, but fans and friends were not really the same thing.

Damion still smiled at Melbrook. No reason not to. "Yeah, sure. If I ever need any more ideas, I'll come to you."

"Cool. So freaky about that girl who slit her wrists, amirite?"

"Freaky?"

"Just sort of bizarre she'd just come back like she did."

Damion frowned and glanced at Mr. Harris, who was supposed to be monitoring the detainees. He hoped Mr. Harris would put a stop to the conversation. Damion was not feeling indulgent enough to deal with Melbrook.

Melbrook followed his gaze and shook his head. "You clearly don't spend time in detention if you're worried about talking. The only rule is no phones. We can read, study, talk, paint nails . . ." He gave a meaningful nod to the corner where a girl was adding an extra layer of ebony to her fingernails. Her black outfit, strategically sliced and stitched back together, was a visual sign that screamed, "Stay away."

"So anyway," Melbrook continued. "It's weird she'd come back to school, don't you think?"

"I don't think I follow. Why weird?" Damion asked. He felt protective of Addison now that he'd met her, talked to her, seen the burden of pain in her eyes. He knew what excess burden looked like, what it felt like, and he wasn't in the mood to let anyone take potshots at Addison.

Melbrook shrugged. "They say suicides happen in threes. She comes back like this, she might give other kids the idea to . . ." He mimed slicing his own throat and then lolled his head to the side with his tongue hanging out.

"I don't see her coming back that way at all. I think it's brave that she showed up. And she's a nice person who cares about other people. She's not part of some subversive underground handing out leaflets to a mass poisoning party."

"Dude, calm. I was only—"

"Well only *don't*. She's my friend. I care about her, and I'm not going to let anyone trash on my friends."

He said the last bit louder, making everyone look at him. Mr. Harris obviously didn't approve of spirited discussion as he shushed Damion in a long, leaky balloon kind of way. Damion pictured an animated version of Mr. Harris deflating in detention.

"Dude. Did you even know her before she did this to herself? You say you're friends, but do you ever hang out? Go to lunch? Go to the same parties?"

Maybe it was the direct messages that had bled over into comments online, but Damion fixed Melbrook with a hard stare. "Do *we*?"

"What?"

"All those things you just listed. Do we hang out, go to lunch, go to parties? You say I'm *your* friend. Are you telling me it's not true? Are we not friends? Are you lying to people when you say you're friends with me? Because I've heard you tell people that we're tight, man. So . . ."

Melbrook's pale skin blossomed into a tomato red that matched his hair. "That's not what I meant. I just—"

"She's my friend. And I will trash on anyone who says differently."

Melbrook lifted his hands in surrender. "Okay, fine. I wasn't trying to pick a fight." After a few minutes, he added, "We're okay, right? Still friends?"

Damion felt like he'd achieved an Olympic-level victory by not rolling his eyes at the guy. "Yeah. Still friends." He definitely felt like Addison Thoreau was closer to being his friend than Melbrook would ever be.

Thoughts of Avery filled his head again, and he felt a smile tug at his lips. She didn't run around telling people she was friends with Damion Archer because she thought it would make her look cool or anything. She didn't name-drop or act like his relationship with her was something it wasn't. She was real with him all the time. When she'd been nice to him earlier, he knew she'd meant it. When she'd been mad and narrowing eyes at him, she'd meant that too.

He considered all the ways the day had been a surprise. He'd surprised himself when he'd thrown himself against the laundromat door, fully expecting to have to fight armed dealers in order to break her out of there.

The relief he'd felt when she'd been safe?

Definitely a surprise.

That he kept thinking about her and wanting to check in with her and see how she was doing?

That was the biggest surprise of all.

He pulled out his sketch pad, not to storyboard—he never did that when other people could see. His animations were never made public until the final product was uploaded to his account. He sketched out a quick rendition of Avery standing out in the snowy field. Something about the way she'd stood out there in the cold made her seem so vulnerable.

"Nice drawing," Melbrook said, peeking at the picture.

"Thanks." Damion had almost forgotten where he was as he layered in the highlights and shadows. Having an audience made him glad he'd left the details ambiguous so no one would recognize the girl he'd drawn.

"I thought you only did cartoons. I didn't know you could do real art."

Damion ground his finger over the graphite, smudging it harder than he needed for the bit of shading he'd created. "Animation *is* real art." Why did people say things like that to him? "Different mediums and styles don't validate or invalidate the craft."

Melbrook stammered something that might have been agreement, but it wasn't the apology it should have been. He went back to minding his own business.

Damion inspected his handiwork before the smile tugged at his lips again.

He wondered if Avery would be willing to spend another lunch hour with him. Would she scoff and tell him to get over himself? Or would she smile and agree? He had the feeling she'd ask him if he'd lost a bet. Or she'd say yes and then say it was because *she'd* lost a bet.

"Hey!" Melbrook said. "Did you see this?" He moved his phone from where he'd been peeking at it in his lap and slid it to where Damion could see.

It was a comment on Damion's latest YouTube video: *I can't believe this guy. He uses people at school for likes and fame. Total faker. Anyone who subscribes to his channel is a follower in more ways than online.*

Damion stiffened, trying not to reveal the way he felt about such a comment. Wasn't it bad enough he had to read these on his own? Did other people really need to point them out to him?

"Dude, people suck sometimes, amirite?"

"Yep. Haters suck for sure." Damion pushed the phone away, but as he looked at Melbrook's face, he thought he saw a glimmer of something that made his lungs tighten. Triumph. Vindication. Satisfaction.

Melbrook, the guy who always claimed Damion as a friend, seemed only too happy to grind Damion's face through the mud of spiteful comments. That was the problem with followers. They wanted to claim your friendship while you scaled the cliffs in front of you, but even more, they wanted to watch you fall. They wanted to be there, waiting at the bottom with everyone else so they could comment on the significant splat you made when you hit the ground.

Melbrook clucked his tongue. "It's hard to be famous, I guess."

"Not really," Damion responded. "What's hard is dealing with people who are bitter about their own mediocrity."

When Melbrook looked down as if ashamed or embarrassed, Damion caught Mr. Harris's eye and gave a barely perceptible nod in Melbrook's direction to make sure Mr. Harris saw the contraband.

"Is your phone out *again*, Mr. Melbrook?" Mr. Harris was quick to step down the aisle, his hand held out for the phone.

Melbrook blustered. "But, Mr. Harris—"

"You were warned." Mr. Harris snapped his fingers to hurry along the handoff.

Damion didn't feel better for his passive-aggressive revenge. He thought about the message Melbrook had shown him and the satisfaction in Melbrook's eyes. Maybe Damion was already in a free fall to the ground. Maybe it was too late to fix anything.

Should he call it quits and get serious about college? He couldn't do that, though. His personal nightmare at home barely allowed room for high school and the time he spent creating his videos. It didn't allow room for anything as intense as college.

Maybe this was the place where Damion was rolled over by the combination of his success and his demons.

He frowned and tucked his sketchbook away.

If people knew his truth . . .

But they didn't. And it wasn't anyone's business but his.

:⋆* 16 *⋆:

Addison's Journal
December 7, 3:11 p.m.

I left my last class of the day as soon as the bell rang with the hopes of simply escaping, but Hazel was waiting by my locker. I can't avoid her the same way I've been avoiding Booker.

Especially since she'd been crying. Why is everyone crying today? She wanted to know if I hated her. Wow. I am so messed up, and I have so messed up the people closest to me. I told her that I didn't hate her. At. All.

She cried because she said she felt like maybe I did what I did because she was spending so much time with Liam, which simply isn't true. I like Liam. He and Hazel are adorable together—like they're starring in their own charming high school rom-com. At least in a good one. Some movies get everything about high school wrong.

Anyway, I told her a dozen or more times that I love how happy she is and that my issues are not her issues at all.

But it's not true.

I lied.

Because my issues *are* her issues. At least they feel like they are.

It's why I haven't been able to talk to her. She was doing fine until I lost my mind. My actions have consequences for others—not just me. She visited me in the hospital with mascara streaming down her face and her eyes puffed out like she'd been crying for days.

That was the thing I realized when it was almost too late. If I had succeeded, it wouldn't have just been something I did to myself. It would also have been something I did to everyone who cared about me. I threw a huge boulder into the ponds of their lives, not just rippling the water but splashing it all the way to their farthest shores.

The therapist is good at her job. Good enough that she and I have argued this before. She's told me all the ways I'm not responsible for other people. Maybe I'm not. But I *am* responsible for me. If I want people to *see* me, then shouldn't I try to see them too?

I don't have answers. Maybe when I graduate from therapy.

So I hugged Hazel while she cried. I am not responsible for her. But I am responsible for how I treat her. She is my friend. I will treat her gently. That's how it works.

* * *

Avery

Avery started making dinner for everyone who would be home that night. She never cooked for more than herself except on special occasions like her dad's or Tyler's birthdays, Christmas Eve, and Thanksgiving. Everyday, sit-down family dinners were a thing for television, not her real life.

She usually didn't mind that her family was what they were. She liked not having to worry about anyone else for meals. But for whatever reason, with this new girl and her baby occupying her brother's bedroom, she wanted to make a good impression even though she felt pretty sure she was being *extra*. She wasn't even sure why since to hear Jo talk, she likely never had sit-down family dinners either.

Which meant Jo wouldn't be throwing shade.

But it wasn't just wanting to impress Jo or make her comfortable. Avery needed to butter up her father too. What would he say when he found out she was harboring the sister of Tyler's rival drug dealer? She hoped the baby would help keep her father rational and calm about the whole thing. A baby and dinner? Her poor father wouldn't know what hit him.

He'd been a walking disaster since her mom died. She sometimes felt amazed he got himself dressed and out the door in the morning. And when Tyler had spiraled entirely out of control and started the lying, jackbag behavior that was Tyler, her dad's equal parts pathetic and apathetic behavior became worse.

Her family was jacked up. That was the whole story of it. So why was she trying to impress a girl whose life was just as jacked up?

She didn't have a satisfying answer, even though she kept circling back around and phrasing the question in different ways in case she'd come up with an answer.

She'd picked one of her mom's old recipes after determining they had all the ingredients—sort of. It was a chicken mixture wrapped in rolls and then rolled in cornflakes. She had no intention of attempting to make the rolls from scratch like the recipe called for, and she had some canned crescent rolls in the fridge.

And though they didn't have cornflakes, she did have Rice Krispies—well, the generic version of Rice Krispies anyway. They were a month past their expiration date, but they didn't taste stale, which was a huge plus, and once they were crushed, it would be close enough that no one would know the difference. Probably.

While she prepped the food, she kept thinking about what Jo had said about Tyler and his depression. And about her and her own. Shortly after their mom had died, her dad had taken both her and Tyler to a grief counselor. He'd gone too. They had a few sessions, and he then figured that was that. But it hadn't been. Not for her or Tyler.

Her phone buzzed with an incoming message. She felt a flutter of something she couldn't quite identify as she smiled and looked down, expecting to see a message from Damion. It wasn't from Damion. It was from a number she didn't recognize, which made her naturally wary considering her brother's drug rival's sister was hanging out upstairs.

"I'm sorry I missed earlier."

She squinted at the message as if that would help her understand it better. She almost typed "Who is this?" when a new message came through.

"This is Celia."

Celia! She had forgotten. She'd been tutoring Celia in math, which was why she'd been carrying the pre-algebra book Damion had given the stink eye to earlier. The morning felt like a million years ago. Forgetting Celia meant she'd stuffed her brain too full of real life. She was glad Celia hadn't been waiting around in Mrs. Armstrong's classroom for Avery to show up; at least Celia didn't know Avery had totally blown her off.

"No worries," Avery texted. *"See you tomorrow?"*

There was a long wait before her phone buzzed again. *"I don't think so. My schedule is kind of up in the air. I'll let you know when I'll be available for tutoring."*

"Tell me about up in the air," Avery said out loud to her kitchen.

She felt relieved at being off the hook for tomorrow as well.

She had a lot of stuff going on, and though she knew Celia needed the help—and Avery was getting extra credit for being her tutor—she didn't know how to fit one more thing in, at least not until she got her current situation figured out.

She threw her head back and squeezed her eyes shut. "I'm an idiot," she muttered.

She had told Damion to take her and Jo and the baby to her house rather than back to school. She hadn't given a second thought to the classes she would miss. Not that she could have hauled Jo and a baby to school. How would that have worked out? She hadn't even thought about the fact that her motorcycle was still in the school parking lot.

Avery had done the only reasonable thing that could have been done. But she felt like garbage about it. Celia was brilliant in history class, and she did all right in English, but math was Celia's poison. She'd failed it once before, and she wouldn't graduate if she couldn't pass it. Mrs. Armstrong had chosen Avery specifically as Celia's tutor.

Avery had let her down by skipping out—not that Avery would have known that since Celia was also a no-show.

Convenient.

"You okay?" Avery texted after thinking about it for several minutes.

"Sure."

The immediate reply felt suspect, but what could Avery do? Demand details from this girl she only sort of knew?

She considered typing something about being available if Celia needed anything, but a wail pierced the silence of the house. Startled, Avery put her phone down and looked up at the ceiling. It was a good thing she hadn't tried to keep Jo and baby

Tyler a secret. She'd had no idea a little person could make such a big noise.

Not too long after the wail turned to silence, Jo came into the kitchen with baby Tyler balanced on her hip.

He had a chubby fist stuffed into a slobbery mouth, and his big eyes watched Avery as intently as she watched him.

"Sorry," Jo said. "Sometimes he wakes up grumpy."

"Well, he's got that in common with his dad." Avery smiled to take the bite out of her comment.

"Say hello to your Aunt Avery," Jo instructed Tyler.

Aunt Avery. That was a phrase that would take getting used to.

The baby gurgled, and a half smile appeared around the fist.

Avery smiled back, instantly charmed by this little guy who was part of her family. When her mom died, her family shrank both literally and figuratively.

It never occurred to her that families could grow too. Experience had only taught her about shrinkage and loss. But apparently families expanded as well as contracted, like breathing.

She put out her hand for the baby, and he removed his fist from his mouth to grab hold of her finger. He gripped hard, which forced her to move closer to him and Jo.

"He likes you!" Jo said with a laugh.

Avery eyed where her hand and his connected. She liked him too.

She thought about how much her mom would have loved this little guy in her kitchen. And for the first time in forever, she felt lighter, healed in ways she hadn't ever imagined.

Would her father feel that same healing?

She took a deep breath and hoped.

Because she knew what it had been like after her mother

died. Her dad had become hard and sharp all at the same time. It was part of what made Tyler rebel the way he did. Would his hard and sharp come out when he saw another piece of evidence of all the dumb things Tyler had done?

She glanced at the clock. He'd be home in just over two hours. Ready or not, she'd find out soon enough.

17

Addison's Journal
December 7, 3:42 p.m.

Mom couldn't pick me up because of work. She had one of her friends, Piper, come get me, which meant I spent the entire ride listening to her detail all my mom's sufferings and how worried she is about my mom. Her comments were also loaded with pretend concern for me.

I normally like Piper, but I didn't need the extra helping of guilt. I have enough to supply the entire state of Massachusetts.

Piper didn't drop me off when we got to my house. She came inside and insisted she'd stay until my mom came home.

I really wish she'd leave.

. . . .

Booker

Booker wanted to rush to Addison's locker as soon as school was out, but he wasn't stupid. The way she'd slipped in and out of classes like a ghost meant there was no way he'd make it to her locker before she disappeared.

149

Knowing that, he took his time finishing his assignment, turning it in, and gathering his stuff. He refused to allow himself to look for her in the halls. She wouldn't be there. And he wouldn't let himself drive to her house and demand answers. She wouldn't give them to him if he did. But even if he thought she would give them, he didn't want to cause her turmoil, especially as a result of something he did.

Besides, he'd promised his mom he'd pick up his little brother after school and haul him to hockey practice. He couldn't chase the shadow that was Addison all day.

At the junior high, his brother hopped in the car and slouched low in the seat.

Booker frowned at him. "What's the matter, Nater-Tot?"

Nathan rolled his head along the headrest of the seat and glared at him. "Don't call me that."

"Right. I forgot. You like Tor-Nate-O better."

Nathan grunted as he rolled his head back over the headrest to look out the window. "Just drive."

"You didn't pay for this ride, so you can't order me around with the threat of leaving me a bad rating, but because you look seriously bummed, I'll let it slide." Booker pulled into traffic and turned toward the ice rink. "What's wrong? Seriously."

Nathan looked at him, his dark curly top reminding Booker that he'd soon be losing his own hair. "No teasing?"

"No teasing," he promised. If he was being honest, he didn't feel like teasing anyway.

"I don't get girls."

Booker let out an involuntary laugh and immediately regretted it when his brother shot him a look of betrayal. "Sorry, buddy. I'm not laughing at you. I'm laughing because it almost sounded like you were hoping I would enlighten you on that topic."

"But girls like you."

"Not all girls, Nate-O." He waited for Nathan to explain what, exactly, was so troubling about the girls in his life. When he didn't, Booker poked for more information. "So, this is about a girl you like?"

"Maybe."

More silence.

"Does she like you?"

Nathan shrugged.

"Who's the girl?"

Another shrug.

Booker pulled into the ice rink and parked behind an oxidized Hyundai so old it predated the turn of the century and had been through several hailstorms if the dents were any indicator. It was Hazel's old beater.

His brother sucked in a hard breath when Hazel's younger sister and brother hopped out from the back seat. They were twins, and Griff played on Nathan's hockey team. Hazel must have been on driver duty too.

Hazel looked happier than when he'd last seen her that morning. How could they still be on the same day when it felt like a week had passed? Hazel clicked her key fob, making the headlights flash. She turned and saw Booker, lifting her hand in a cheerful wave.

Nathan's eyes widened as Hazel, her brother, and her sister headed their direction to walk inside with them.

Booker glanced from his kid brother to Hazel's little sister, AJ. A few things clicked into place. His brother was feeling girl-angst, and now, here they were with a girl he refused to make eye contact with even after she said, "Hello, Nathan."

He bumped his brother's arm, trying to inspire the kid to speak up. If Nate liked her, ignoring her wasn't going to help his situation.

"Hey, AJ." Nathan still refused to look at her. He swallowed like he had a mountain lodged in his throat.

That proved Booker's theory. They'd found the girl in question.

Mystery solved, little brother.

"'Sup?" Nathan said to Griff, and the two walked into the rink together, their hockey bags knocking into their legs. AJ looked disappointed.

Booker would have to give Nathan a little direction once he got the kid alone.

"So, you look better," he said to Hazel as they followed the two hockey players into the rink.

She flipped her long, black box braids over her shoulder and smiled. "I am *so* much better."

He gave her a meaningful look—one that hopefully inspired her to keep talking.

"Addison was at her locker after school, and we—"

"What? She was?" He wanted to kick himself. If he would've gone to check instead of being irritated with Addison, he might have the same peaceful look Hazel wore.

"Yeah. I was glad I caught her because it looked like she was trying to hurry. But we talked, you know? And it's just been so long since we talked I thought it would be all awkward and stuff. But it wasn't at all. She's not mad at me. She likes my boyfriend and says she's happy he and I are together, so we're good, you know."

He nodded, feeling a little stupid for being jealous that Hazel had some resolution he missed out on.

"What about you?"

"Me?" He gave a brief laugh. "That question is lemon juice squeezed over a paper cut."

Hazel winced. "Sorry."

"Don't be. I'm glad you had a better day, and I'm glad Addison knows she has you."

"You should let her know she has you, too, you know? You could tell her you like her. I think she'd really be happy to know that."

A hot spark flared up in him, burning with anger, frustration, and pain. Wasn't that what Booker was trying to do the day in the library?

He'd just wanted her to know that he liked her. Really liked her. Up until the moment she ran away from him, he'd thought she liked him too.

He shook his head. "I don't think that's a good idea."

Hazel came to a stop and then tapped AJ on the shoulder. "Run in and get us seats. Top of the bleachers so we can lean against the wall, K?"

AJ darted ahead, leaving Booker and Hazel standing alone on the sidewalk.

"Tell me. Why is being honest with Addison *not* a good idea?" Hazel asked.

"I don't think she wants me to like her."

"That doesn't even make sense."

"I tried to let her know that I liked her. Before. But she freaked out, and the next thing I know, she's in the hospital."

"What?" Hazel's eyes widened. "Spill the tea. Tell me

everything." She crossed her arms and tapped her toe and waited for him to confess.

He ran his hand down his face and looked around to be certain no one could overhear them. He was tired of wondering. Maybe if Hazel knew everything, she could help him, and together they could help Addison.

"We weren't even on a date." It was a weak beginning, but how else could he begin? "We were killing time in the library during lunch." He frowned, reconsidering talking to anyone about his fears.

"And?"

"And nothing! We were pointing out our favorite books to each other and just having fun. Everything was perfectly normal. And then we moved deeper into the stacks where the librarian couldn't see us, and Addison looked like—"

"Looked like what?"

Hazel looked like she might pound him into paste, which meant he had to finish the story before she took a swing at him.

"She grinned. You know, in a way that said she liked being with me as much as I liked being with her."

"And?" A polar bear would have needed a jacket under the freezing tone of that one word.

"And that grin just looked . . . kissable. So I reached out and tucked her hair back behind her shoulders and leaned in. That's it. I expected her to meet me halfway. I thought she liked me too."

"Did you kiss her without her permission?"

"'Course not. My mama taught me better than that. I didn't kiss her at all."

He hadn't closed his eyes in anticipation of the kiss, but that only meant he saw exactly the way her eyes widened in terror.

He'd jerked back at the same time she did. He'd been baffled. Had she been scared?

Of him?

How could she possibly be scared of him? They'd been friends for years, all through high school and most of junior high.

"If you didn't kiss her, what happened?"

"I don't know. She looked at me like I'd grown fangs and horns and a tail and said, 'I'm about to cut open your head and eat your brains. Doesn't that sound nice?' But I swear I didn't do anything except touch her hair and lean in. Her reaction was just . . . troubling."

He'd watched her shrink into herself, and that had been the worst.

Booker's volunteer work at the animal shelter helped him understand people better. He loved animals—dogs, specifically—and a lot of them came through the shelter with that same protective posture he'd seen in Addison.

Crouched. Huddled. Like they were trying to hide from something bigger than they were.

"Then?" Hazel prompted, looking as confused as he felt.

"Then nothing. She bolted. Without a word. Just fled as if her life depended on it."

Sympathy replaced Hazel's fury. "Ouch."

"Yeah. Ouch." At first, Booker had been bewildered. What. The. What? Then he was hurt. Then he was angry. But he wasn't angry for long because he recognized the panicked look on her face.

The dogs at the shelter sometimes came from terrible circumstances after having suffered abuse or neglect—things that were kind of unspeakable. So for Addison to have that same look, that same wildness in her eyes, had to mean she was dealing with something awful. But why take it out on him?

"What did you do then?"

He shrugged. "Nothing. I figured I'd let her sort things out and then we'd talk. But she ditched school the next day. I thought about calling her, but she was obviously working through some crap, and I didn't want to get in the way. And then she—"

AJ came around the corner. "Are you guys coming?"

Booker felt relieved by the interruption. It gave him a moment to get it together.

"In a minute," Hazel called to her sister. "Did you get our seats?"

"I had to scoot over a lady with a purse dog, but I did what you told me."

"Awesome. Thanks. But you need to stay there, or the lady with the purse dog will swipe our spot. Go back."

AJ groaned but did as directed.

"Sorry," Hazel said.

He shrugged again.

"It's not your fault, you know." She echoed the words he'd told her that morning by the lockers.

"Then why did she run?"

It was her turn to shrug. "Did you need a stick of gum? Because no girl wants to kiss a guy who smells like he gargles garbage."

Booker narrowed his eyes at Hazel. Maybe she wasn't the best person to confide in. "Bad breath? You think she ditched me because of bad breath?"

Hazel blew out a breath and uncrossed her arms so she could shake out her hands. It was a nervous gesture. She did it before she had to speak in front of the class for oral reports too. "I guess not. It's obviously . . . well, someone should talk to her about it. Do you want me to?"

Booker shrugged, hating that his shoulders were more conversational than the rest of him.

"We should *both* go talk to Addison. Tonight," she said.

"I can't."

She narrowed her eyes at him. "Oh, okay, then. If Addison isn't that important to you, I guess this conversation is over."

"Wow. Judgmental much? I'm getting a haircut tonight." His heart felt like someone was squeezing it from inside his chest. He imagined it was how bigger dogs felt when people used collars that were too small: constricting, suffocating, painful.

"A haircut? You're choosing a haircut over helping a friend?"

He turned away, intending to go to his car and drive away before he remembered he had to wait for Nate to be done with practice.

He moved back and glared at Hazel. "I don't have to take this from you, Hazel. You have no idea what I'm going through, so maybe stop assuming I'm some kind of villain. What I'm choosing is my family. My cousin has cancer. He starts chemo tomorrow. We're both shaving our heads. Is that a good enough reason for you?"

Hazel's irritation vanished, and tears swam in her eyes as she put a hand on Booker's arm. "I'm so sorry, Book."

Before she could say anything more, AJ popped up from around the corner again. She glared at them. "You're supposed to be in there with me!"

"I'm coming!" Hazel insisted, tightening her grip on Booker's arm and dragging him into the rink.

The temperature dropped as they got closer to the ice. The sounds of blades snicking against the ice and hockey sticks tapping in the quest to control the puck filled the silence between Hazel and Booker as they marched up the bleachers to their seats at the top against the wall.

"I'm sorry. I didn't know," Hazel said finally, her eyes on the practice taking place on the ice. When she looked up at him, her mouth formed a sad downward turn. "Your hair though . . ."

He was glad she saw the loss for what it was. He would miss his curls too. "I invited Addison to come tonight. She said no." He didn't know why he'd blabbed that. It made him feel disloyal. Like he was tattling.

"You could ask again. Maybe send a text?"

He shook his head. "No. She looked at me like I was a mutant and told me she couldn't make it. Anyway, she doesn't care about me. She's practically in a relationship with death; why would I think she'd support my cousin's fight for his life?" It was a bitter thing to say. He hated himself for saying it. "But even with all that, I'm still worried about her. I don't want anything bad to happen to her. I just . . . I don't know what to do."

He didn't know why he kept blabbing all his insecurities, irritations, and fears to people. First Damion, now Hazel. If he kept this up, he'd be shouting it all over the loudspeaker during morning announcements in school. He needed to pull himself together.

Though Hazel frowned, she also nodded. They sat in silence for a few moments. Then she called out, "Go, Griff! You got this!"

They sat in more silence.

"I'll talk to her tonight," Hazel finally said. "Check to make sure she's okay."

Relief flooded him. He hated how all over the place he felt emotionally. He was simultaneously worried for and extremely irritated with Addison. At least if Hazel talked to her, he could let go of some of the worry.

"What time are you lopping your locks?" Hazel asked.

"Eight thirty." He rubbed his hand over his head and tried not to let panic rise in his chest. It was just hair. Big deal, right? "Make sure you talk to her," he said after a moment. "I know you guys talked earlier, but . . . I dunno. I'm just worried about her."

He knew he'd still worry even with Hazel talking to Addison. He would worry because he cared about Addison. He *liked* her.

He wanted her to keep breathing.

But he was afraid that no matter what he did or didn't do, Addison might try it again. He didn't know what he would do if woke up one day and Addison didn't exist in the world anymore. He'd never be able to handle it.

18

Addison's Journal
December 7, 4:27 p.m.

I think my mom's friend Piper hates me. I swear she hasn't stopped glaring at me since we came into the house. Piper didn't used to hate me. She used to call me things like "Babycakes" and "Sugardoodle." Now she uses my actual name, and she does it like it's her new favorite swear word.

She hasn't said it, but I know what she's thinking. She's thinking I'm the reason for my mom's misery. And I know. I know what I put my mom through. I also know Piper means well. She's looking out for my mom, but seriously? What's up with that? Because . . . she has no idea what's going on with me. Who is she to judge? Was she there all those times when that man hurt me? Was she there when my mom and I had to flee in the middle of the night? Did *she* have to leave everything she ever knew behind because an adult who was supposed to protect her hurt her instead?

I need to calm down.

What would the therapist say?

She would tell me to calm down.

She would tell me that I don't know what Piper's life is like either and that maybe Piper has struggled with things I don't understand.

She would tell me to be patient with Piper in the same way I want Piper to be patient with me.

I swear the therapist is good at what she does if I can hear her voice so clearly in my head. Or maybe I've just lost it and this other voice I hear is a fracture of my consciousness that still has a handle on rational behavior.

Not possible.

If some part of me had been rational that night, where was it when I did what I did?

Wouldn't a rational part of me have interjected at some point?

I hope Piper will stop looking at me like I am the biggest disappointment the world ever produced.

She doesn't understand.

How can she?

I don't understand.

• •

Celia

Sophie smiled wide, as if Celia joining her in the kitchen to help make dinner was as awesome as a trip to Disney World— not that Celia knew anything about Disney World. For a long time, her mom promised they would go, saying that if Celia made dinner every night and kept the house clean, they would go—just the two of them.

Fact: They never went.

Her mom always blamed Celia for it. If dinner was burned because her mom came home later than she'd said, her mom would say, "I guess you didn't really want to go to Disney World or you wouldn't have ruined dinner." If the house had been perfectly spotless when Celia went to bed but then trashed when she woke up because her mom invited a boyfriend or a few friends over to drink, her mom would say, "I guess you didn't really want to go to Disney World or you would have done what I'd asked instead of letting the house get so filthy."

I guess you didn't really want to go to Disney World or you would have . . .

Fact: Disney World opened in 1971. Even though Celia wasn't even alive when it opened, she felt like she'd wanted to go since they first opened their gates to the public. That's how bad she wanted to go.

"Does it make you cry when you chop onions?" Sophie asked.

Celia blinked, having forgotten where she was and what she was doing for a moment. "Onions? No. They don't bother me."

"You sure? 'Cause onions make my eyes sting for a good hour after the meal has been eaten. So I wouldn't fault anyone for being afflicted in the same way."

"I'm sure." Celia washed her hands and took the onion from Sophie. She set it on a marble cutting board and stared at it a moment while she gripped the knife in her hands. "Excuse me," she said. "How do you want them cut?"

"We're doing stir-fry, so bigger slices will be just fine."

Celia began to carefully slice, part of her afraid she was doing it wrong. Her mother had never watched her make dinner, only complained about it when it was done. Complained she had to wait too long for it. Complained it was too dry or too salty or not salty enough. Complained it was always the same boring thing. Celia agreed with the boring part. She didn't know many recipes and fewer still her mom was willing to eat. Add that to the fact that the cupboards were pretty sparse, and it didn't leave a lot of room for variety.

But sometimes her mom ate all the food without complaining. Sometimes she took second helpings and smiled.

"I thought onions didn't make you cry," Sophie said.

"I guess I was wrong." Celia pulled a paper towel from the roll and dabbed at her eyes, and then, hoping she could deflect the attention from her to the food, she asked, "Are these okay?"

Sophie peered over at the slices on Celia's cutting board. "Perfect. Want to do the carrots too?"

"Sure."

"Just do them into little coins." Sophie handed off two carrots. "So tell me about yourself. What do you like to do?"

"Do?" Did she have anything she liked to do? She used to have a neighbor friend—Gary. He was nice to her most of the time. He lived down the street and had a bike he'd let her borrow from time to time. She felt free and alive while on that bike with the wind in her hair.

"I like biking," she said, feeling normalized with the words. Biking was something normal people did and enjoyed.

"That's fantastic. Like mountain biking or regular road biking, or do you do BMX stuff?"

Celia frowned. Sophie knew way more about the sport than Celia did. "Regular biking, I guess," she said.

"Do you have trails that you like best?" Sophie pulled a glass dish with a snap-on lid from the fridge. She opened the lid and dumped the contents into a large wok. The cold chicken sizzled in the heated wok.

"It's nice along the Nashua River Rail Trail."

"How do you discourage mosquitos from making a picnic out of you?"

Celia smiled at the comment—she never would have thought to ask about that. "If you go fast enough, they can't land. It's not such a fun trail when you're just walking." She had ridden that trail so many times she could retrace it in her mind. "Sometimes I go from the trail over to the old burying ground."

"Wow, seriously? Alone? Isn't that far?"

Celia shrugged. "It's only about ten minutes or so on a bike."

"Did it ever make you nervous being around creepy graves like that?"

"They don't seem creepy to me." She wondered if that was the wrong thing to say. Back before Gary moved and took his friendship and bike with him, she would go to the cemetery and walk along the gravestones and think about the people under the grass and leaves. She wondered how they felt about the lives they'd lived. She wondered if it was nice to sleep without worrying about anything. She envied the people under the ground sometimes.

She looked down at the sleeves of the hoodie she wore. *Addison's* hoodie. Was it possible Addison envied the people under the ground as well? The fact was that Celia might once have followed in Addison's footsteps. She'd thought about ending her life a million times a million.

Except she didn't think like that now. Not after Addison had given her a shirt and told her to tell her truth.

Now she felt possibilities creeping in that had never existed before. She felt safer. She felt like she wanted to stick around and see how her future might play out.

"Do you like mushrooms?" Sophie asked as she handed Celia a red bell pepper to slice.

"Yes."

"How about broccoli?"

"I like that too."

Sophie chopped mushrooms and broccoli, and Celia felt almost like she'd stepped into a grocery store because that was the only place she'd ever seen so much fresh produce at the same time.

Sophie asked all kinds of questions. She wanted to know what movies Celia liked, what foods she liked, her favorite subject in school. History was her favorite, but talking about school make Celia think about her least favorite subject.

Fact: Math hated her. She was pretty sure it was personal. How she couldn't pass a class that everyone else breezed through she didn't know. Without her tutor's help, she would probably never graduate.

That was when she remembered she'd been supposed to meet with her tutor, Avery, that afternoon. But between Mrs. Mendenhall, Monica, the doctors at the hospital, and now Sophie, Celia's day hadn't exactly gone like she'd planned.

Celia asked to borrow Sophie's phone. Sophie handed it over, though she seemed a little wary about it.

Celia fished Avery's number from the front pocket of her backpack and texted her.

Avery then asked if Celia was okay. Celia considered the question. Her life was up in the air, but she thought she might be okay. The fact that Avery had asked made Celia's eyes burn with unshed tears again. Avery had always been nice to Celia.

As Celia handed back the phone, Sophie said, "You need a new backpack."

Celia looked at the mangy sack with the broken strap and hanging-by-threads outside pockets. "It's fine," she said.

"It's not fine. I have several. Come pick one out while dinner finishes cooking."

Celia wanted to protest, but Sophie had already left the

kitchen and seemed to expect Celia to follow. She would have wondered what kind of person kept multiple backpacks, but she'd already seen the dresser full of brand-new clothing and the bathroom full of brand-new personal products.

She followed Sophie to a side room where Sophie opened a closet. There were half a dozen backpacks in a variety of colors—black, pink, navy blue, forest green, orange, and red—all with tags still on them.

"Pick your favorite."

Celia wasn't normally a bold-color person. She kept to muted darks because they made it easier to disappear into the background. Maybe it was because the entire day had been so different from any other day in her life, but she chose the red one with a white, asymmetrical spiral cutting through it.

Sophie smiled. "That was my favorite too."

They went back to the kitchen to finish dinner. Celia wondered if Sophie hated how much of the conversation she had to pull from Celia. She wondered what the other kids who'd ended up at Sophie's house were like. She wondered where her mom was. Had they already arrested her? Was she sitting in jail somewhere? Was she angry at Celia, or worse, did she not care enough to be angry?

The more questions that came to her mind, the harder it was for her to answer Sophie's questions. She wanted desperately to go to bed, to burrow into blankets, and not think or wonder at all.

But Elijah, Sophie's husband, came home, clomping into the kitchen as noisily as if he were ten people. He kissed Sophie and then turned his attention to Celia. "Looks like we have a visitor."

Elijah was a big and bold and bald Black man. He didn't

look anything like her dad. Her dad had a full head of hair that used to be blond but now was more of a weird in-between color that wasn't quite blond but not quite committed to brown either. His hair was like his personality—not committed to anything. She didn't know why Elijah's entrance made her think of her dad, and she tried not to think about it.

Sophie introduced them and then gave Celia instructions on how to cook the rice while she pulled Elijah into another room.

Fact: It's rude to eavesdrop. Even with her less-than-perfect upbringing, Celia knew that much. She resisted for a few moments while she finished getting the rice ready. After all, she'd been asked to do a chore, and what would they think if they came back and she hadn't done it? They'd call her lazy. They'd—

No.

Sophie wasn't her mother. Elijah wasn't her father. They wouldn't do anything to hurt her. Still, after she took care of the rice, she crept quietly to the doorway and listened.

"Wow," Elijah said. "She's had it rough, then."

"Monica emailed me saying they're trying to get in touch with her dad. They're hoping to get her settled with him." Sophie's voice sounded like she was holding back enough tears to flood a city.

That intrigued Celia. Had anyone ever cried for her? She didn't think so, and it made her feel warm and loved as well as awkward and uncomfortable.

"What kind of dad leaves his child with a woman willing to burn holes in her arms?" Elijah sounded angry.

Celia felt protected and also vindicated. Hadn't she wondered that same thing a million times a million?

"I know. But we need to be positive for her while we're talking to her. I just wanted to fill you in on what this little soul has endured. We'll find out more tomorrow, but Monica said Celia will probably only be with us for two days. Maybe three."

"Got it. No getting attached."

Sophie laughed softly. "You say that every time."

"It's because if I don't remind myself every time, then I get all mopey when they leave."

"You don't always get mopey."

It was his turn to laugh. "True, but I do with the good ones."

"Celia's a good one. Lots of stuff going on behind those eyes. She'll have a bright future if the adults in her life get their crap together."

"The bright ones are the hardest because we know what their futures can be, and it's awful when that potential fizzles out. The best we can do is show them the amazing people they are and hope that somewhere in their minds they remember."

Sophie agreed.

When a few breaths went by without any further conversation, Celia hurried back to the rice cooker and acted like she'd been watching it and not listening in at all.

It felt good to hear Sophie call her good. And to say there was a lot going on behind her eyes? Was Sophie saying she was smart? It sounded like that's what she meant. And no one had ever said she had a bright future ahead of her.

Her dad used to say she'd turn out just like her mom, and her mom always said she was worthless.

"It sure smells good in here, Celia," Elijah said when he and Sophie reappeared in the kitchen. "You must do a lot of cooking."

Celia shrugged, finding it hard to come up with out-loud words again.

Elijah didn't seem to mind. "Sophie's a good cook too. I

used to think I was pretty good until Sophie told me my cooking wasn't her favorite thing."

Sophie laughed. "Listen to you, acting like I insulted you. The truth is, Celia, he makes an excellent sous-chef."

Celia didn't know what a sous-chef was, but she smiled.

The couple bantered back and forth in a way Celia had never seen before. They carried a lot of the conversation, which made it easier on Celia because she had a lot to think about.

They were contacting her dad.

Fact: She didn't know how she felt about that.

Even after she slipped upstairs to escape the awkwardness of trying to keep up a conversation with strangers, she still didn't know how she felt about that.

19

Addison's Journal
December 7, 5:02 p.m.

Hazel showed up on my doorstep. I don't think Piper was too happy about having a visitor, but she didn't say anything and let Hazel come inside. I was grateful to have the buffer of another person between Piper and me.

At least I was until we went into my room and closed the door and Hazel started talking.

She knows.

About the abuse from when I was a kid.

I never told her.

After my mom and I fled, I never told anyone until I started talking to the therapist. She has encouraged me to talk to my mom about it so many times—since Mom already knows—but I haven't been able to do it.

And now Hazel knows.

How does she know?

She's in the bathroom right now, and here I am, scribbling furiously in this stupid journal as if it can somehow offer me advice or help me know what to say or how to act. I didn't deny it because it's Hazel. Best friends don't lie to each other. But I didn't explain it either.

I don't know how I can explain it.

Maybe when she gets back from the bathroom, I will tell her. How much do I tell? How many details are enough to make her understand without opening the wound too wide and ending with me bleeding out emotionally?

· ·

Damion

Damion glared at his sister's blue Honda minivan in his driveway and took a deep breath before he turned the knob to his front door. He barely had time to close the door behind him before his sister called out, "Damion? Is that you?" She rounded the corner and fixed him with a glare of her own. "Where have you been? I've been waiting for hours!"

"Nice to see you, too, Palmer. I got detention."

She placed her hands on the hips of her yoga pants patterned with Christmas-tree lights and tossed back her dark hair that contrasted with her pale skin. She'd obviously missed an appointment with her hairstylist because her gray roots were showing. "And you couldn't have called? Seriously?"

He moved farther into the house. It wasn't like he could turn around and leave no matter how much he wanted to. "It was detention. They don't allow phones in detention."

"You could have called before that."

"Look, Palmer, I'm here now. What's the big emergency?"

"I've been watching Mom for hours, and I need to go home and make dinner for my own family."

He didn't bother reminding her that her husband did all the cooking at her house because she was possibly the worst cook in the country—maybe the world. Her idea of cooking was takeout. And he resented the way she phrased it as if she'd made dinner for him and their parents. She hadn't ever cooked for them before, and he would bet every subscriber he had on YouTube that she hadn't started tonight. Besides, weren't he and their parents her own family too?

He ignored her play for pity and pushed past her into the living room, where his mom sat folding hand towels in her chair.

The towels didn't need to be folded, at least not as many times as he felt certain his mother had folded them that day. It was what her nurse referred to as necessary busywork to help his mom feel useful.

He wanted to go greet his mom and give her the flowers he'd drawn for her while he'd been stuck in the waste-of-everyone's-time the school felt was appropriate discipline for being tardy, but Palmer grabbed his arm.

"Don't walk away from me."

"You said you'd stay later today so I could work. It's why I didn't worry about calling you when I ended up in detention."

She had the decency to turn slightly red, but she didn't back down. "It's not my fault you wasted the time by screwing around all day."

"I was in school and then in detention."

Palmer let go of his arm and put her hand to her head. "Which is exactly my point! What are you doing getting deten-tion?"

He wanted to yell at her but knew the noise would only make his mom afraid. "I got it because I was late for school again because I was making sure Mom got her pills this morn-ing, and she knocked over her juice and started crying. Dad was in the shower. I wasn't about to leave her while she was crying."

If Palmer had slightly reddened before, she was full-on fire-truck red now. "I've been here all day—"

"You mean 'all day' as in from one this afternoon when Dad had to leave for work until now, which is barely after five? So four hours means all day?"

"And by work you mean draw cartoons for the internet."

"My job is more stable than yours."

"I don't have a job."

"Exactly." He crossed the room but stopped before he reached his mom. Beneath his feet was a blue rug over their beige carpet. He turned back to Palmer. "Why is the rug back?"

"Mom likes blue."

"She might, but the occupational therapist said it was a tripping hazard. If she falls again, she might break a hip or something. You can't redecorate the house every time you come over. The rug can't be here."

"The last time she fell, it wasn't the rug's fault." Palmer said it like an accusation.

He had to force down his anger. The last time Mom had fallen, Damion hadn't even been home. Palmer had. But it didn't matter. What mattered was that his mom had stopped folding and was watching the two of them with tears in her eyes. Any arguing in the house always upset her and made her sad for hours, long after she could even remember there had been anything to be sad about.

He shot Palmer a look over his shoulder that he hoped conveyed every bit of irritation he felt toward her. Then he turned to his mom. "Hi there," he said brightly. "How are you doing?"

Her smile edged out his irritation and replaced it with warmth, at least until she said, "Well, aren't you a handsome young man!"

He tried not to let his smile falter as he leaned down and kissed her cheek. She didn't remember him today. She usually recognized that she somehow knew him, even if she wasn't sure how, but there was no recognition in her eyes at all today.

"Thanks, Mom," he said to help remind her that he was her son. Her eyes widened as if the news of him being her kid surprised her.

She took his hand in her own and squeezed. "You're a sweet boy."

She didn't use his name. She couldn't. He remembered vividly the last time she'd said his name without prompting or reminding. He had painted her favorite vacation spot—a little pond across from their cabin in Upstate New York—and she'd been so excited to receive the painting. "Thank you, Damion. I love it so much," she'd said.

Hearing her use his name had been all the gratitude he'd needed.

"You're a sweet mom," he said to her now.

Anyone just looking at her would have no idea anything was wrong. She was only fifty-six. She wasn't old enough to have Alzheimer's. That was supposed to be a disease for people in their eighties or something.

"I need to go." Palmer cut into his thoughts. "I'm really sorry, Damion. I tried to call Bryson, but it just goes straight to voice mail. I'll come spend an hour or two on Saturday to make it up to you."

He nodded. They were all at the end of what they could handle and hitting their heads against the same wall. Sure, Palmer had been unusually awful and attacked him as soon as he walked in the door, but he knew she was stretched pretty thin too.

It didn't stop him from resenting the fact that she got to go home and catch her breath while he had to stay and watch his mom dissolve. His live-in, all-the-time reality was a place she only had to visit.

"I'm sorry," Palmer said again. She clearly wanted a verbal acknowledgment so she didn't have to feel guilty for leaving.

He nodded again. "Have a nice day, then," he said brightly because he knew it would irritate her, and he wanted her to feel a little guilty since she'd been such a witch. All he wanted now was for her to fly away on her broom.

She made a noise in her throat that could have either been exasperation or a curse, but she moved him out of the way so she could hug their mom. "Bye, Mom. I'll see you soon, okay?"

"Bye, Palmer, baby. I'll see you soon."

Damion gritted his teeth against the jealousy that rose in his throat. Of course, Mom remembered Palmer. She'd married at nineteen and had Palmer at twenty and Damion at thirty-nine. He'd been what his older brother and sister called an accident and what his parents called a wonderful surprise. Sometimes he wasn't sure whose version told the actual truth. His late arrival in her life meant an earlier exit from her memory.

It sucked.

Palmer left, and Damion invited his mom into the kitchen to hang out with him while he made dinner. She followed him and sat at the table. The way her hands moved in her lap like she was flicking away an unseen pest made him wonder if she felt unhappy. *He* certainly felt unhappy.

The school day had been rough, and he would've given anything to come home to a mom who could listen as he griped about how detentions were stupid, how anonymous online comments made it hard to concentrate all day, and how it was stupid that Palmer insisted she needed to take care of her own kids when her oldest was barely three years younger than Damion.

But he couldn't unload any of his mental carnage on his mother. She got worse when people around her were unpleasant. And if he made her worse, they would both be in for a bad night.

"What do you want to listen to, Mom?" he asked. *"Phantom of the Opera? Fiddler on the Roof? Les Mis?"*

She smiled at the last one, her lips looking faded and thin. If she had her full mind, she'd be wearing lipstick every day in varying shades to match her mood.

He streamed the music from his phone to the kitchen speakers and turned the volume up to almost full. She liked her tunes loud.

She laughed in delight. "It's like you read my mind."

She applauded as he acted out the scenes to the songs in between mixing things together for a coconut-ginger chickpea soup. It had lots of curcumin in it. He'd read that curcumin was good for people with Alzheimer's. He'd gotten good at making soups. Everything just went into one pot and then simmered. It would have been easy to get sick of the same sort of meal all the time, which was why Damion worked to make sure no two flavors happened in the same week. Almost every type of meal had a soup version.

When he heard his dad's car pull into the garage, he breathed a sigh of relief. Entertaining his mom all on his own exhausted him, and he still had to finish storyboarding his next video.

His mom heard the sound of the garage as well and rubbed her lips together before frowning.

"No worries, Mom. I got you." He pulled a lip balm from

his pocket and handed it to her. It was tinted a light burgundy. He picked it because the color was called Red Dahlia, and that appealed to him at an artistic level.

He'd stopped feeling bad about tricking his mom into thinking she was applying real lipstick a long time ago. What worked, worked. And the bonus of such a minimal tint was that if she missed and smudged it a little, it didn't hurt anything and she didn't end up looking like the Joker. He was pretty sure his dad had been relieved when Damion had thrown out all the lipsticks and bought the lip balms.

He wished Palmer understood the importance of the lip balm. He'd tried explaining that it made their mom happy, it made her feel like she still had some control over her life, and it made her feel pretty. Palmer had all but patted him on the head for being such a cute little dim-witted boy, and their mom always had pale, dry lips when Palmer was in charge.

His dad entered the kitchen through the garage entrance, placed his messenger bag and keys on the counter, and grinned wide for both of them.

"There's two of my favorite people!" he said as he strode to the table and kissed his wife.

At that moment, a direct message notification chimed on Damion's phone. Damion didn't check to see what it was. He knew it was the same troll who had been sending him messages all day. He didn't know how much more hate he could take.

"Dinner smells good, buddy." The compliment pulled his attention back to the kitchen and his parents.

He looked up to see his dad eyeing the pot on the burner. He likely hadn't eaten anything since breakfast, which had probably only been a bowl of cereal and maybe some toast. Damion swelled under his dad's praise, but not as much as he would have if he hadn't felt sure that whatever message waited for him on his phone would not be kind.

"Thanks, Dad. I'm going to eat in my room if that's okay. I have a lot of work to do tonight."

"I thought Palmer was staying late so you could get work done."

"Yeah. I thought so too." He didn't say anything else because he didn't think he could do it without being a jerk. Palmer did what she could do. He couldn't blame her for not understanding what it was like living in the same house with it, for not understanding what it was like to wake up with Alzheimer's looming over everything, or what it was like breathing it in all day and then going to sleep with it again. And it's not like he wanted her to know. He wouldn't wish his reality on anyone.

When he was in his room with his door closed and his soup on his desk next to his graphics tablet, he finally took out his phone and clicked on the message.

"U R disgusting! Did U have fun faking friendship with the suicide girl? Everyone knows U R a faker, a fraud, and a no-talent loser. But don't U worry. Someone is going to blow UR life up. Watch UR back! Even at home. Cause we're watching U!"

Damion's blood pounded in his ears. He yanked out his chair and turned on his laptop. He went to the various social media platforms being used to troll him to see on a large screen what kind of profile had been created for the accounts sending him direct messages. On all of them, the account's profile picture was either his own yearbook picture with a red slash through it or a picture of his logo for Inside-Out Archer covered with poop emojis.

"And this moron is calling me a faker?" he murmured out loud to his computer screen. He'd been reporting and blocking messages and accounts all day, but new accounts kept cropping up.

He should have been working. He should have been creating another video. Instead, he took his soup back to the table and sat down by his mom.

"I thought you had work to do," his dad said.

"Yeah. Well, I guess I just need to be with my parents right now."

While he talked with his dad about college—a topic that likely surprised him—and the prospect of learning more regarding animation, he thought about the fake accounts and the threatening messages. He worried this mystery person or people might genuinely know where he lived.

What if they did? What if they showed up when he wasn't home and hurt his mom? He nodded as his dad talked, smiled for his mother, and gritted his teeth against his anger and worry.

20

Addison's Journal
December 7, 6:23 p.m.

Hazel listened while I talked. She really listened, and I talked way more than I ever imagined possible. Way more than I have ever done with even the therapist. I explained so much, and yet I feel like I didn't explain anything at all.

She hugged me so tightly before she left I almost couldn't breathe, but now that she's gone, taking my secrets with her, I feel like I'm breathing better than I have in years. She only left because my mom came home. She asked if I wanted her to stay, and I did, but I know my mom wants to talk about school and how the day went, and I owe her that much.

My mom seemed like she wanted Hazel to stay because it seems normal and she likes it when I seem normal, but I can't have Hazel there holding all my secrets while I try to explain my day with Mom. It had to be one or the other. I was glad Piper left too.

I am writing while Mom makes dinner. I should've thought about making dinner. It would have given Piper one less reason to grumble about me, and it would have made Mom's day so much easier.

Tomorrow.

I will make dinner tomorrow.

That's progress, isn't it?

Believing in a tomorrow?

I should have believed sooner. I should have told someone besides a therapist my secrets sooner.

All those years ago, Mom and I left practically everything. My toys, my clothes, my stuffed owl. Everything. Her things too. All we took were some important legal documents, a crystal bowl that was her mother's, and some photo albums that she later meticulously combed through to delete any hint of that man from our lives. She made sure we could not resurrect him with so much as a sock.

But for all her work to bleach our lives, how could anyone have guessed that the touch of someone entirely unconnected to him could bring him back with such force?

Maybe it makes sense.

I have lived for years with this secret burning me up from the inside. I wanted to hand it off to someone else, to hold it out and beg them to take the fire from my hands so that I could find some relief. But I didn't. I tucked it deep inside myself and let it burn.

And burn.

And burn.

Until it seared my insides and left my soul in a pile of ash at the bottom of my heart. I've been choking on the ashes every time I take a breath. For years.

If I had handed off my personal inferno sooner, would I be going on dates with Booker like a normal person?

The sad truth is that I will never get the chance to rewind and do over.

Will I?

Avery

"Hi, Dad," Avery said as soon as he walked through the door and hung his coat in the front closet. He kicked off his snowy, wet shoes while he was still on the tile and entered the multi-shaded-brown carpeted part of the living room.

"Hey, kiddo. It smells good in here. You wouldn't have made enough to share with your old man, would you?"

She smiled brightly. "Actually, I did. I thought it would be nice to have a sit-down family dinner."

"Our family's a little small for formality with just the two of us, don't you think?"

"I might've agreed with you this morning, but . . . Could you sit on the couch with me for a minute?"

He raised a graying eyebrow that was encroaching on the space above his nose. "Am I going to be unhappy with you?"

"I hope not. But I'm serious. We need to speak quietly. Pretend the government is listening."

"You put one of those digital assistants in our home so you could listen to your music. The government *is* listening."

"Okay. That's probably true, but do you promise?"

He flopped down on the couch. He'd clearly had a long day. "Okay. I promise."

Just then, baby Tyler let out a cry that was shushed pretty quickly, all things considered. Jo was incredibly attentive as a mom.

Her dad, who had been slouched into the cushions, sat up straight. He eyed her with suspicion. "Is there a baby in our house?"

"Don't freak out."

"Where did you get a baby?" His eyes widened. "Is it yours?"

Avery snorted and rolled her eyes at her father. "While I think I'm pretty talented, do you honestly think I could hide a whole pregnancy?"

"Your brother hid his drug dealing."

"Right." Avery took a deep breath. This wasn't going smoothly at all. "About that . . ." She explained the situation so quickly the words slurred together, and she worried her dad didn't understand.

One look at her father's murderous face, and she knew he understood better than she'd given him credit for.

"Dad, you promised you'd talk to me. You promised it would be done quietly. I do *not* want you hurting her feelings. Jo's a nice person, and the fact of the matter is that whether you like it or not, Tyler has a kid. Which means you have a grandson."

That last word stopped her dad as he moved to stand up, probably to stomp upstairs and unleash on Jo all the anger and disappointment Tyler had caused him. He lowered himself back to the couch and put his hand to the side of his head as if he'd been slammed with a killer headache. "Okay. I promised. Start talking."

Avery glanced to the stairs and began again, this time explaining everything in greater detail.

He took it pretty well, all things considered. He'd spent a long time being furious with Tyler, but he wasn't such a tyrant that he'd hold an infant accountable for what his stupid, jackbag dad did.

"So she can stay? They can both stay?" Avery asked, feeling like she'd been through a battlefield over the course of the conversation.

He didn't commit but instead said, "I'd like to meet my grandson and his mother now if you don't mind."

Avery wanted to kick her dad for making this whole thing harder on her by not giving her a straight answer, but she nodded and jumped off the couch, then took the stairs two at a time to go collect the people in question. She hoped Jo had the baby in more than a diaper because more than once, she'd heard her father criticize people who took their kids out in public in the equivalent of underwear. She probably should've warned Jo about her dad's weird prejudices.

She didn't need to have worried. When she knocked on Tyler's door and then opened it, she saw Jo holding baby Tyler, who wore blue dinosaur-print footie pajamas. Both baby and mother were ready to be put on display.

I am so not old enough to be brokering this kind of relationship, she thought as she smiled at Jo and hoped she looked reassuring.

"He's excited to meet you," she said.

Jo's wide eyes and tight lips showed she didn't exactly believe Avery. But there was nothing more Avery could say to make her feel better. There was nothing more to do except go downstairs and let them find their own comfortable together.

She'd already decided she wasn't going to let her father kick Jo and the baby out. They were her family now, and that was that. She would make her father see.

Avery led the way down the stairs and, at the bottom, stepped aside so her dad and Jo faced each other directly.

His eyes went straight to the baby.

And they filled with tears.

Avery hadn't seen her father cry since her mother's funeral. She didn't know he had any tears left.

"Dad," Avery said, "this is Jo, Tyler's girlfriend. And this little guy is Tyler. He was named after his father."

Baby Tyler must have known how much this first meeting mattered because he tucked his head under his mother's chin and smiled shyly at Avery's dad.

"You named him Tyler?" her dad asked.

Jo nodded.

"How old is he?"

"Four months."

"Can I hold him?"

Jo relinquished the baby, who went willingly to Avery's dad. The baby apparently didn't know the importance of "stranger danger" yet.

But once Tyler was in her dad's arms, the baby happily melting himself into her dad's shoulder, Avery stopped worrying about whether or not her father would let them stay and then began to worry that her father might never let them move out.

Her dad was a lot like Damion. As he held baby Tyler, he asked Jo questions about herself. Where she went to high school. What her favorite subjects were. What she wanted to do as a career someday. What she thought about college.

Avery remembered dinner was ready and so guided them all to the dining table so they could continue talking but also get some eating done. She instructed her Google assistant to play some Christmas tunes and turned the volume to low so it filled the background without intruding on the conversation.

Jo asked questions too. She wanted to know all about Avery's dad—and about her mom too. At first, Avery cringed when Jo asked how Avery's parents had met. Her dad didn't talk much about her mom. It made him too sad. So it surprised her when he answered.

"We were in line for popcorn at the movie theater. I noticed her standing behind me, and I knew she was way out of my league. But I got the last of the popcorn. When the kid at the counter told her it would be a few minutes while they made more, Lisa said she'd end up missing the beginning of the movie if she waited. She mentioned she was going to *The Mummy*, and it just so happened that so was I." Avery's dad ran a finger over his mouth. "I don't know where I got the nerve, but it just came out. I told her I'd share mine if she wanted so she wouldn't miss the beginning. And, fantastically enough, she agreed."

Everyone laughed. Avery knew the story, but it had been so long since she'd heard it she felt as if she were hearing it for the first time.

He continued. "She had friends there, so she hurried to tell them she was sitting with me, and that was that. She ate more than her fair share of popcorn, and she laughed at all the right places in the movie. When she laughed, it sounded like home." His voice cracked, and he cleared his throat.

Avery had never seen her father click with someone so quickly. And she hadn't heard him talk to anyone about her mom at all since her mom had passed away. She looked between Jo and her dad and felt her heart fill and expand as though it had taken a deep breath of love. In the background, the music of "O Holy Night" swelled to its finish.

After dinner, Jo cleaned up while Avery's dad walked around the living room, bouncing the baby and showing off the Christmas-tree ornaments by pointing and saying, "See the white star? See the blue icicle? See the red Santa hat?"

Avery watched her father in open amazement. Had he ever been that guy? The kind who cooed and burbled and practically fell all over himself to make a baby giggle or smile? She did not know the man bounce-walking and singing Christmas carols in a thin, out-of-tune voice. It was adorable but so irregular she wasn't quite sure what to make of it.

A text came through on her phone, distracting her from her thoughts. She hoped her dad didn't see the way she reacted to that text because she was pretty sure she was grinning stupid and blushing hot.

It was from Damion. *"You are more than welcome."*

He was responding to her thanking him for his help earlier. She hadn't thought he would. She read the words several times over to see if he was just being polite or if he meant anything else, which was futile because those five words could not mean anything more than what they said.

Another text came in. *"Are you busy tonight?"*

She was more than busy. She glanced at her dad dancing to "Jingle Bell Rock" with the baby and thought about Jo in the kitchen cleaning up. But was she really beyond all reason busy?

"Depends. I don't do fan meet and greets."

"😄 Please remember I'm the comedian here."

She grinned at her phone. *"That might be the case, but I'm not going to drive the getaway car while you knock over a convenience store or do a drug deal either."*

"If I call you princess like a certain YOU did to me earlier, how much trouble would I be in?"

"So. Much."

"Figured. Anyway, this isn't for me or about me. There's this guy, Booker. He's friends with Addison Thoreau. He's shaving his head tonight for his cousin who has cancer. He asked me to come, but I figured he wouldn't mind if I brought a plus-one."

Avery's dad's voice broke through her thoughts. "What has you frowning at your phone like that?"

Avery tried to clear her face from the emotional confusion she felt. Damion Archer was going to a head-shaving party? "You ever feel like everything you knew was wrong?"

He settled himself on the couch next to her, his breath coming a little hard and fast from the exertion of dancing a baby all over the room. "You mean like thinking I was just a dad and now I'm a grandpa?"

She smirked at him. "Oh, come on. You know you are so much more than *just* a dad."

"Nice." Then he nodded toward her phone. "What's up?"

"Do you remember Damion Archer?"

"Archer . . . Archer . . . Didn't you steal his go-kart?"

"Is no one going to let that go?"

"Is he finally pressing charges?"

"He asked me to go to a head-shaving party—not to shave my head!" She hurried to interject the last at his immediate look of disapproval. "A kid from school is shaving his head because of cancer."

Jo came into the room, reminding Avery that leaving on Jo's first night in their house was a jackbag thing to do.

"Never mind, Dad. I can stay."

"What's going on?" Jo asked.

Avery's dad explained what Avery wanted to do.

"You should go," Jo said to Avery.

"But it's your first night here and—"

"And you should go. I'm just going to get Tyler ready for bed and then going to sleep myself." Jo looked to Avery's dad. "We're all good here, right?"

"We're all good here."

That settled that.

She texted Damion back. "*Okay, what's the address?*"

"I'll come get you."

She knew Jo, her dad, and baby Tyler were all watching. So she refused to smile on the outside.

But she couldn't keep her insides from grinning.

21

Addison's Journal
December 7, 8:10 p.m.

Hazel updated her Instagram with a picture of her wearing a mullet wig that she's taking to Booker's head-shaving party. That's the theme, I guess—everyone is supposed to bring a comical form of fake hair. If I were going, what kind of hair would I bring? A mophead? That wouldn't work. We don't use those kinds of mops.

Why am I even thinking about it? It's not like I'm going. Booker will be surrounded by friends and family. Me showing up would be stupid. And awkward. And stupid awkward.

I'm surprised Hazel is going. I am the thing that connects Hazel to Booker. It stings a little to think of them hanging out without me. I don't know why. It just stings.

I did the dishes to make up for Mom doing dinner. She seemed grateful even though she protested for nearly five whole minutes saying I needed to rest. She's the one who went to work today and needs to rest. I barely existed, which means I don't need to rest.

She finally gave in, and I was glad. I need to do something useful, something that adds to everything around me rather than drains it all away. She stayed in the kitchen with me while I did them, though.

And even now she is sitting on the couch while I'm sitting in the overstuffed chair by the Christmas tree. She's watching me, but she's pretending she's reading. I know she's pretending because she hasn't turned the page in fifteen minutes and she reads a lot faster than that, especially when she's got a book she likes. The one in her hand is a Regency romance. I can tell by the woman in a white, high-waisted gown on the cover. Romances are her favorite. If she was actually reading, she would be turning pages.

Not that I can judge. I am sitting here commenting on her watching me when clearly I am watching her, too, or I wouldn't know how long ago she turned her page.

I wonder what the therapist would say about that.

Hazel commented on the heart emoji I left on her picture of the mullet wig. *"I can come get you if you want to come. The mullet can be from both of us."*

She said that exactly. Why would she think I would want to go?

Do I want to go?

No.

Yes.

Maybe?

• •

Booker

Booker glanced around his living room. His mom had made all kinds of cookies, brownies, and cupcakes, along with providing drinks for everyone. She'd also made healthy snacks because that was how she handled everything in life. Balance.

She took care of all the details for the party because Seb's mom, her sister, was overwhelmed with grief over her son's ordeal. That was how his mom said it: *overwhelmed with grief.* They all were.

Seb, oddly enough, was pretty calm about the whole thing, as if cancer was a blip in his life. No big deal. He was the one smiling at everyone, making everyone else feel comfortable with his situation. Booker didn't know how he could be like that, how he could walk around clapping people on the back, offering hugs, extending the comfort that people should have been giving him.

Under normal circumstances, the decorated room and table of food would have looked like a regular, everyday Christmas party, but the four chairs in the middle of the room and four sets of hair-cutting tools told a different story. There were four sets because Booker wasn't the only one showing solidarity with Seb. Seb's little brother, John, was shaving his head too, and so was Daniel, Seb's best friend from his high school.

The plan was that they would hang out, eating cookies and taking pictures of their fabulous locks, then Seb would open the wig gifts. After that, they would fire up the razors.

Since it wasn't time yet and most people had yet to arrive, Booker felt weird. He couldn't describe it better than that. Why weird, though? He didn't have to make any of the food. He wasn't in charge of anything.

He didn't know why he felt panicked about the whole thing. It was just hair, but his hair was a source of pride and comfort for him; it was the kind of appreciation he knew many people like him were not allowed to feel about their natural hair. The last thing he wanted to lose was that pride and comfort. Well, no. The last thing he wanted to lose was his cousin.

Seb had been his best friend since the beginning of everything. Seb's family had lived down the street for a lot of years until his dad got a job transfer. Booker worried he would lose Seb's friendship, but that hadn't been the case. The internet, texting, and phone calls kept them as close as ever. Then they both got their driver's licenses and could drive to see each other whenever they wanted, and it was back to business as usual.

This party felt like they were making a joke of something that scared Booker more than the time he almost fell off the roof while hanging Christmas lights.

Seb grabbed Booker's shoulder. "Man! You said your bae was coming to watch you fall from the Rapunzel tower."

Booker's anxiety spiked. He hadn't told Seb about Addison's attempt. Booker hadn't told him about anything that caused him personal stress or worry because what Seb was going through was a million times worse than anything Booker was handling. And how could he explain about Addison? He couldn't, so he'd kept it to himself.

But now? Did he lie? Did he avoid the topic by changing the subject?

"Yeah, she's really going through it. Been out of school for a while, so she's trying to get caught up. And she's not my bae. We're just friends, you know?"

Seb lowered his voice and grinned at Booker. "My man, you're not gonna play the 'just friends' card with me. I have heard you go into long and exhausting detail on all the ways this girl is *the* girl. So what happened?" Seb's face sobered. "Did she dump your sorry butt?"

"'Nah, bro. We were never together, so there can't be a breakup. Like I said, she's missed a lot of school. It's complicated." An image of Addison's frightened face before she ran from him, before she ended up in a hospital, flashed through his mind. Complicated was the only way to describe that situation.

"Sorry. But don't worry. I've got girls from my school coming, and I'll definitely introduce you to some of them."

"Only some?"

Seb grinned and lifted a shoulder. "I'm generous, not stupid."

The doorbell rang. His mom opened the door to a blast of frigid air and welcomed a group of five people Booker didn't know. They came in, shedding coats, hats, and scarves and then immediately rushed over to Seb. They all talked at once, acting as though they were at a party celebrating something awesome instead of something awful. They had packages wrapped in Christmas paper, and a few of them tried to hand the gifts to Seb.

"I'll take those," Booker said.

Five boxes were immediately piled into his arms, and he managed to keep hold of all of them as he took them to the table next to the food and organized them along with all the others.

He took his time.

Why am I being an idiot? Up until the group of five had arrived, he'd felt weird, but he was surrounded by family—aunts and uncles and cousins, his brother, his parents, his grandma. Comfort people.

He didn't know these people from Seb's school. He wished Matt hadn't been getting his wisdom teeth out so he could have someone who was there for *him* specifically. He'd invited Damion, but the chances of some random famous person he'd just met showing up at his house were exactly zero.

"I can't believe I invited him," he murmured.

"Invited who?" Seb was right behind him with his friends.

Booker turned, shoved his hands in his pockets, and smiled. "No one."

Seb introduced his friends.

They all gave their names, but Booker, in his frantic state of mind, forgot the names as soon as they were said. As it turned out, the guy wearing Christmas slippers was an exchange student from Germany. He thanked Booker for letting them all come to his house and lifted his hand.

Booker gave him a knuckle bump and smiled when the guy snapped his fingers at the same time Booker did. Seb must have taught his friends, and for some reason, that made Booker feel calmer.

Booker's mom took a picture of them, which resulted in everyone posing and cheesing for his mom's camera. From there, everyone pulled out phones and snapped group selfies. The doorbell rang and rang and rang. Seb's friend group grew with every chime. There were a lot of bald jokes, "no more bad hair day" jokes, and laughing. Booker laughed too.

Even though the gallows humor settled wrong in his soul.

He downed a cup of citrus-infused water and ghosted around the fringes of Seb's friend group. The doorbell rang again, but his mom was busy restocking the food tables, so Booker answered it, expecting to see more of Seb's friends.

Damion and a girl Booker didn't really know but had seen around at school stood on his porch.

"You're here," Booker said, unable to keep the surprise out of his voice.

"I'm assuming my invitation didn't expire or anything?" Damion said.

"No. Of course not."

"Does that mean you're going to let us in?" Damion gave a meaningful nod to the fact that Booker was blocking the doorway.

Booker stepped to the side. "Sorry. I was just surprised to see you, that's all."

Once they were inside and Booker had taken their coats, Damion pointed at the girl with him. "This is Avery Winters. I figured you wouldn't mind if I brought her."

Avery said hello, but her eyes trailed to the table with all the wrapped presents. "Were we supposed to bring something?"

Booker shook his head. "Those are mostly from family and Seb's friends. It's kind of a freaky-wig contest."

"You're really going to cut off your hair?" Avery asked him.

He shrugged. "It's just hair." And with Damion there to support him, it felt true. It was just hair.

"It's just great hair," Avery said. "I think I might cry for you."

Booker laughed, drawing Seb's attention, so Booker took his friends over to introduce them to the guest of honor.

When Seb heard Damion's name, he did a double take. "Damion Archer? As in Inside-Out Archer?"

Damion tucked his head in his shoulders slightly as if to say "Guilty as charged."

Seb thumped Booker on the shoulder. "Man! You're friends with Damion Archer, and you didn't tell me?" Before he let Booker respond, he turned back to Damion. "I loved the winter camp survival episode. Seriously. Loved it."

Seb's friends all agreed. Seb grinned every time he looked Damion's direction in almost hero worship. Booker considered how weird it was that he and Seb were such good friends and yet Seb had never sent Booker a link to Damion's channel. He'd never even heard of Damion Archer before today, let alone known the guy went to the same school. It was one more weird thing that made no sense in his life.

"Is Addison coming to watch you lose your head?" Avery asked.

"It's not the French Revolution, Avery," Damion said. "I doubt they have a guillotine out back."

The weirdness Booker had been feeling returned in full force. Though he laughed at Damion's joke, he wondered how Avery knew of his connection to Addison. Did everyone know? He wondered if Hazel had made it to Addison's house to talk. He hoped so. He hoped Addison was doing okay.

"Are we talking about the girlfriend my cousin denies even exists?" Seb asked.

All eyes—and several knowing grins—were now on Booker. "She's got a lot going on. She can't make it," he said. If Seb didn't have cancer and Booker didn't feel devastated at the thought of losing him, he'd have killed his cousin for making girlfriend jokes in front of the whole crowd.

Luckily, his mom and aunt called everyone over to the fireplace to get all the photos Aunt Summer wanted.

Booker ended up tucked between his cousin and Avery for pictures.

"Hey," Avery whispered, tugging at his arm.

He leaned his head down so he could hear her above everyone laughing and suggesting different pose ideas for the group.

"Addison's lucky to have you as a friend. It's something I've been thinking about all day. Just thought you should know."

He felt his jaw drop, and then he heard the click of his mom's phone taking a picture.

22

Addison's Journal
December 7, 8:13 p.m.

I have looked at Hazel's message on my phone a hundred times. She makes a good point. I can't hide forever. Not that she actually made that point in so many words, but she sort of hinted at the point enough that I'm pretty sure it's what she meant to say.

I did a search for homemade wig ideas. There were the standard mop and yarn wigs, but there were also ones made out of all kinds of things I wouldn't have ever thought of—lace, repurposed baskets, pantyhose. Seriously. Who even thinks of pantyhose? Who under the age of eighty even owns pantyhose? People are creative. Bizarre but creative.

I didn't have it in me to get all crafty and create something that wouldn't embarrass me. I almost decided to give up. It's not like I'm going. But then I saw a design made out of paper. I could make something out of paper.

My mom gave up pretending to read. She asked me what I was doing. I told her without explaining the details. And she didn't ask me any more questions. She just went in search of the types of paper and other supplies I'd need.

I keep telling myself I'm not going to Booker's party, but then, why am I making a stupid wig? Maybe I will give it to Booker at school as an apology for not being there for him when he needed me. And I know he does need me. I saw the desperation and pain in his eyes when he asked me if I was still going. His cousin is to him like Hazel is to me. Asking me for some support made him vulnerable. And what did I do with that? Shot him down.

I owe him a homemade art project when I see him again.

It is the least I can do.

After everything else, it's the very least.

· ·

Celia

Celia sat on the bed with the white bedspread and stared at the new socks on her feet. Her mind raced for ways to fit the pieces of her day in an order that made sense to her.

"I blew up my life," she said to her socks.

They didn't have a response, which was, in fact, a relief. She felt like she'd lost her mind. Talking socks would confirm her fears.

How was she supposed to recover after blowing up her world?

What was her mom thinking? More importantly, what did she think of Celia?

She hated that she couldn't stop asking herself what her mom thought of her. How many times had she asked it that day? A million? A million times a million? Her math wasn't good, but she was pretty sure it had been at least that many times.

They'd called her dad.

What does he think of me?

That question was easier, though it didn't make sense. She

figured she'd always known he hadn't really liked her, or he would have taken her with him when her parents split up, or he would have asked her to stay on those few times he had her come to visit. He would have known she was being hurt and come and saved her. Wouldn't he?

Celia shook her head and abruptly stood from the bed.

She picked up the new red backpack from the floor by the bedroom door and then grabbed her mangled excuse of a backpack from where it sat by the bed. She slid back the white comforter to empty her backpack contents on the sheets underneath, but they were as clean and brilliant white as the bedspread was. Her belongings would not keep such clean bedding white.

She slid down to the floor and emptied her old backpack, shaking out every loose penny, bent paper clip, and folded-up paper. She scowled at the glass shards that glittered on the carpet. It seemed a lifetime ago when the strap broke and her pocket mirror shattered in front of Damion Archer. She'd thought she'd thrown away all the glass but had apparently missed some.

Carefully, Celia picked up each little glittery shard and splinter, grateful the light in the room hit the ground in a way that shimmered off the silvered glass. She moved to her feet to put the pieces in the garbage can she'd seen in the bathroom and yelped.

A red spot bloomed on the bottom of her left sock. She cursed. Had Sophie and Elijah heard her? What would they think?

She limped to the door and swung it open as quietly as possible, but the door hinges squeaked. Sophie wasn't standing directly outside the door, but she was in the hall, and she looked in Celia's direction.

"Are you okay?" Sophie asked.

"I just stepped on a sliver or something." She almost tightened her fist around the broken glass but stopped herself in time. She didn't want to hurt herself even more than she already had.

Even when I'm not with my mom, I get hurt.

"A sliver?" Sophie asked. "Give me a minute, and I'll meet you in your bathroom." She hurried to the end of the hall, where Celia assumed Sophie's bedroom was.

Celia hobbled to the bathroom as directed and hurried to discard the glass fragments in the metal canister next to the toilet. She washed her hands to rinse away any tiny pieces that might have stuck to her skin. She sat on the toilet lid and inspected the place where she was bleeding. She glanced back to the hallway, worried she'd accidentally gotten blood on the carpet. She didn't think she had.

She gently smoothed her fingers over the place where the blood was to see if the sliver was sticking out of the sock but couldn't feel anything. With a grimace, Celia carefully removed the sock and ran her fingers along her skin. Something was definitely sticking out, but even when she squinted, she couldn't see it.

Sophie bustled into the bathroom, placing a first aid kit on the counter by the sink. She pulled out a tiny pair of metal tweezers that had a round window in them.

"Let's see about this sliver, shall we?" She held up the tweezers and looked at Celia as if asking for permission. Celia nodded, and Sophie sat in front of her, took Celia's foot, and set it on her own knee. She flipped a small button on the tweezers and a small light came on, illuminating the place where the tweezers came together. Celia realized the little window was a magnifying glass.

Watching Sophie work fascinated Celia. Not only were the tweezers one of the fanciest things she'd ever seen but Sophie was also working to remove something that hurt Celia, not working to further inflict harm on her. The sliver was out in no time, and, after Sophie rubbed an alcohol pad over the spot, she smoothed a bandage over it.

"This is waterproof and sticks really well, even to the bottoms of feet, but I'll leave a few extras on the counter if you need them."

Sophie tossed the bandage wrapper in the garbage can where Celia had thrown away the glass shards. "Did something break?"

It didn't sound like an accusation, but Celia still cringed. She hurried to explain, her words tumbling out. "A mirror that was in my backpack broke this morning, and I guess I didn't clean it out very good because some pieces fell out when I was putting my things in the backpack you gave me, and . . ." She trailed off, feeling dumb for her explanation.

"Oh." Understanding registered in Sophie's widened eyes. "We should get your room vacuumed up so you don't step on any more pieces."

Celia's chest tightened with a familiar panic. "I don't want to be any trouble. I can just walk carefully."

"Girl, you can't walk carefully enough to avoid glass splinters unless you can float to your bed!" Sophie laughed. "I'm getting a vacuum."

Celia stopped arguing the point and waited by her bedroom door until Sophie returned with a vacuum cleaner. As soon as she reached Celia's room, Celia reached for the handle. "I can clean it. It's my fault. It's my mess."

Sophie stopped and put a hand on Celia's shoulder. "It's okay. You're not in trouble. It was an accident. Accidents happen.

They happen to everybody. They happen to me and to Elijah and to your teachers and to your mom and to your dad. So it's okay if they happen to you too. Do you understand?"

Celia thought she understood.

Fact: Sometimes, accidents made good things happen. Penicillin was discovered because a guy accidentally left out a bunch of petri dishes filled with staph infections while he went away for a while, only to come home and discover the dish with mold in it hadn't grown more of the infection. That accident ultimately saved lives. Not that dropping glass on the floor was a lifesaving event, but Celia didn't want to argue with Sophie.

Whether Sophie was saying it or not, her words made Celia think that maybe her mom was wrong to punish her for little accidents.

She would have to think about that later. "Really, though. I can clean my own messes."

Sophie gave up control of the vacuum handle. She waited until Celia was done so she could put the vacuum away. Celia watched Sophie wrap the cord and felt stupid for not having thought about doing it herself. She never did it at home. She always picked the cord up in one swirled pile and stuffed it all in the closet. It was something else to think about later.

After Sophie left, Celia moved the contents of her old backpack to the new one. It felt clean and organized and ready for something new.

A knock came at her door, and Celia called out, "Come in!"

It was Sophie again. She held her phone out to Celia. "It's for you."

Celia eyed the phone suspiciously. Sophie had been so uncomfortable with her borrowing the phone before. Would Avery be calling her back? No. That would be weird. Avery knew Celia always borrowed phones.

Instead of asking who it was, she took the phone. "Hello?"

"Hi there, Celia. It's Monica. How are you settling in?"

Celia's eyes met Sophie's. Monica. That made sense. "Good. Everything's good. Sophie's real nice."

Sophie smiled and then closed the door to give her privacy.

"Wonderful. She's one of the best. I was calling because we were able to get in touch with your father."

Celia suddenly felt like her heart was trying to pound its way out of her rib cage. She nodded, even though Monica couldn't see her.

"He wanted to talk to you tonight. I have him on the other line and can patch him into this call. Is it okay if I do that?"

It was as if two opposing forces were pulling at her frayed emotional threads, threatening to tear her into pieces. She wanted to talk to him. She hated the thought of talking to him. She needed him. She wanted to prove she didn't need him.

"Celia?" Monica prompted.

"It's fine."

"Okay. Hold on a second while I get him clicked over."

Celia moved to the bed where she could tuck herself under the bedspread, whether to find comfort in it or hide beneath it, she wasn't sure. When she pulled the white cover over her, she saw Addison Thoreau's hoodie. She pulled it close and hugged it to her chest.

This was Addison's fault. Hadn't she been the one to urge Celia to tell? Hadn't she called Celia's life *messed up?*

If it wasn't then, it sure was now.

How do I feel about that? That was something Mrs.

Mendenhall, the school counselor, had asked her. She'd wanted to know how Celia felt about everything.

Fact: Celia didn't know.

"Okay." Monica's voice coming through the phone startled Celia. "Your dad is on the line with us. Celia? Are you still there?"

"I'm here." Celia wasn't sure she'd said it loud enough to be heard.

But then her dad said, "Hey, honey. Are you okay?"

Celia didn't know how to answer that. Yes? No? She didn't say anything.

"They told me what happened," he said when the silence stretched out. "I'm so sorry, honey."

She didn't know what to say to that either. She felt like her throat was all clogged up and keeping her words locked in her lungs.

"I'm coming to get you. I'll be in Massachusetts in the morning, and I'll probably be able to pick you up tomorrow night. If not, then the day after. Is that okay?"

Permission.

He was asking for her permission. How many times had people asked her permission during the day? More than she could count. More than ever before in her life.

"You're coming?" she finally said.

She felt like she'd been strapped into a dilapidated roller coaster and was clacking up a hill with no way of knowing what was on the other side. Were there even tracks on the other side? She wasn't even sure her seat belt would hold her or if it would snap and she'd fall to the ground where she would shatter like her mirror.

"Yes," her dad said in a voice that sounded like he meant it. "I'm coming to get you. Is that okay?"

"I don't know."

He let out a gust of breath that sounded as if someone had punched him.

"You don't even like me," she whispered.

"Baby, that is not true. Not true at all. I love you. And I should've fought for you. I should've fought to keep you with me. And I didn't. I can't make what I did or didn't do right. There isn't any way to go back and fix it, but I can be better going forward if you'll forgive me and give me a chance to prove I love you."

"What about Stephanie?"

"I know you're worried about her, but don't be. Stephanie got a job as a teacher, and she's been seeing students in her classes who have so many struggles in their lives, and she's told me so many times about how they reminded her of you and how she wished she'd done things differently with you and how she didn't know how to reach out to change things in that relationship. We assumed you didn't want us to reach out, but that was a mistake we both made. I am so sorry. We both are. But she is so glad to get this chance with you, to be there for you and grow a relationship with you—if you want that. So, do you want to be with us? Is it okay if I come get you?"

Celia held Addison's hoodie tighter to her and sucked in a breath. She held that breath for a long time before she said, "That's okay."

The words felt . . . like a fact.

23

Addison's Journal
December 7, 8:21 p.m.

My mom is still off gathering paper and things. I don't know what she thinks about this whole thing. But I like that she hasn't asked why I want to do any of this. I don't ask her what she thinks of it. I want to, though. I want to talk to her like I talked to Hazel.

Hazel has texted me twice, asking me if I want a ride to Booker's house. I haven't answered. I want to. But I haven't. Because what do I say?

Booker has dated a lot. He complained once that his parents think it's important for him to date lots of different people so he doesn't get too attached to just one person while in high school. Why am I writing this? I don't know.

Maybe it's because when he started paying a different kind of attention to me than he did the other girls, it felt like it meant something. He looked at me differently than he did those drones.

He told me this story once about how his dad caught him "studying" with a girl who wore a lot of metal bracelets all up her left arm. I think her name was Zoe. Anyway, Booker's dad said Booker would have been in less trouble had he and Zoe cracked open one of their books and at least pretended to study.

Booker had laughed, and then he told me his dad had said, "A pretty face is awfully boring if nothing intelligent ever comes out of it."

It hadn't been weird for him to tell me all that. We were friends. We told each other all kinds of weird things. He then told me how his dad had sat him down and had a long discussion over the types of girls worth spending time with and what kind of qualities they should have.

That was when it got weird.

Because Booker stopped talking and looked at me.

He really looked at me.

He looked at me in a way that made me wonder if maybe he thought about me the same way I thought about him. I remember feeling the flush of heat crawl over my skin like an invading army as he tilted his head as if seeing me for the first time. I know I was red. No way could my face feel so hot and not have turned as red as a tomato.

My face feels like it's that same kind of flushed right now just thinking about it. It was so embarrassing. And yet it was also so amazing.

I had Booker's attention.

Booker always dated girls who *expected* his attention. I wasn't that girl. How could I expect the attention of anyone when I'd spent so long working to be invisible? That's what the therapist commented on. She commented on how it seemed I wanted to be invisible.

Maybe that's why the Booker question was—*is*—so hard for me to face.

I am no longer invisible to him.

Damion

He didn't know what would happen when he'd stood on Avery's porch to pick her up. His hand felt like it had frozen off in the amount of time he stood there with his finger hovering over the doorbell before he actually got up the nerve to hit the button.

He didn't have to wait long before Avery's dad opened the door and let him in. Her dad had the baby from earlier in his arms and seemed like he was pretty happy about that, so Damion assumed everything had worked out okay for Jo and she was going to get to stay.

Once he and Avery were on their way to Booker's house, he asked about Jo and the baby. Then they arrived at Booker's, and with Booker and his cousin and his cousin's friends all consumed with taking pictures, he was basically alone with Avery. He just wasn't quite sure what else to say to her.

"Sorry if being here seems weird to you. I didn't think we'd need to stay for very long. How long does it take to shave a head, anyway?"

They stood by the food table. Avery munched on a caramel-filled cookie that looked so good Damion took one for himself.

"It doesn't seem weird to me." She gave him a sheepish sort of sideways stare. "I think I misjudged you. A lot. You coming out to something like this? Did you see the look on Booker's cousin's face? You made his night by being here."

Damion tightened his jaw. She had it all wrong. "Can I make a confession?"

"Only if you promise it's something truly humiliating for you."

He rolled his eyes at her and leaned against the wall. "Seriously? Did no one go to your five-year-old birthday party or something?"

She leaned against the wall too. Their arms brushed against each other, and he wasn't stupid enough to not notice that he was happy to connect with her if even in the smallest way.

"*You* were at my five-year-old birthday party," she said.

He laughed. "Well, my gift must have sucked because what else could make you so mean now?"

"I'm sorry." Her cheek twitched as she hid a grin. "Wasn't this about you and not me? Weren't you confessing something?"

"I'm getting hate mail."

Several moments ticked by.

"And?"

"And—wait. What do you mean *and*? Hate mail doesn't need an *and*. It's bad all by itself."

"Oh, okay, princess, a world where not everyone loves you is not a confession. It would've made you look pseudonormal if you hadn't ruined it by thinking it was some epic revelation. That was a weak confession." She picked up another cookie and practically shoved the entire thing in her mouth all at once.

"The hate mail started this morning after we talked. That's why I needed to find out about Addison. I thought if people saw me with her, they'd stop calling me a faker, poser, hypocrite—which they spelled wrong by the way. You haven't totally misjudged me. That's the confession."

"Are you saying you're only here because you want people to believe you're a nice guy?" She looked disappointed, which made him feel like he had to explain further because she was getting it all wrong, again.

Or he was telling it all wrong. "No. I'm here because—"

She reached for another cookie, and he grabbed her hand to stop her. "Look, I'm not here for some PR stunt. I met Booker earlier, and he seemed bummed. Like he needed some support. I'm here for him and that's it. And I might've started the whole thing with Addison for the wrong reasons, but now it's different. Besides, I think she helped me more than I helped her. And not because I got PR out of it. Honestly, no amount of PR can help me with whoever has decided to bully me by sending me all this hate."

Avery laughed, which made him wish he'd never said anything. "Bullying? You?"

He released her hand. "Okay, bullying is the wrong word. It's a hundred times worse. I'm not talking your basic hate mail where they're insulting my videos or whatever. Or telling me they don't like my hair. These are personal attacks. Threats. It's getting weird."

Avery shrugged. "I wouldn't worry about it, Archer. People are jackbags. It's a quantifiable truth." She gave him a look that made him think she'd lumped him in the "jackbag" category.

"They left threats, and with my mom's situation, what if they came over and rang the doorbell or whatever, and she answered the door, and they did something to her?"

Avery's demeanor shifted. "What about your mom?"

Too late, he realized his mistake. "Nothing. I just worry that someone disturbed enough to make threats might be someone disturbed enough to carry them out."

"Give me your phone." When he hesitated, she snapped her fingers at him. "Phone, Archer. And stop looking panicked. I'm not going to look through your pictures or anything."

He handed it over to her, not at all trusting she wouldn't do anything damaging. She slid her finger over the screen, scrolling for what, he couldn't say. While she worked, he packed away a few more cookies. He hadn't had Mom-made cookies in a long time. Not since his mom's decline.

"You guys doing okay?" Booker asked.

Damion and Avery had stopped paying attention to the crowd of people in the living room, which meant that Booker surprised him and almost made him drop the cookie in his hand.

"Yeah. We're good. Did your mom make these? They're ridiculous." He almost asked for the recipe but couldn't figure out how to do that without sounding awkward.

"My mom loves baking. Hey, my cousin was wondering if he could get a few pictures with you—just you and him. I don't want it to be weird or anything, so if you don't want to, it's fine, I just thought maybe . . ."

"Of course." He shooed Avery's hand out of the way of his screen so he could use his phone as a plate for his cookies. "Don't be eating those. You get your own. And don't be reading my texts or emails while I'm gone because friends do not do that to friends."

He wiped the excess crumbs on his jeans and followed Booker back to where his cousin stood by the fireplace.

He had a good time in the little photoshoot with Seb. The guy was cool. They reenacted a few scenes from the winter survival camp sketch. At one point, he glanced up to see Booker on the outskirts. The guy's mouth was stretched over his face in the worst fake smile Damion had ever seen.

"Hey, would it be cool if we have a couple with Booker? I want evidence of his savage locks before they're gone. Not that I'm crushing on him or anything, but I'm with Avery when she said she'd be sad to see his hair go."

Seb made a playful *psh* noise. "If we have to, I guess."

Damion called over to Avery. "Would you be willing to take our picture?"

"With what? All I've got here is a cookie tray." She held up Damion's phone with the cookies stacked on it.

Booker's mom hurried over with an actual plate for the cookies and settled them at the edge of the food table. Avery blushed and apologized for not doing it herself, which made Damion laugh. Avery was seriously stunning when she blushed.

He felt his smile freeze on his face. Where had that thought come from?

Not that it wasn't true. It was absolutely true. He just hadn't expected to be thinking it. Especially not in the middle of a crowd when his face had likely gone as red as hers had.

Avery covered her embarrassment by holding Damion's phone in front of her face. He hid his own embarrassment under his practiced half grin as she took the pictures.

The doorbell rang again, and Booker's mom, who had been watching all the photo antics, answered.

Damion recognized the two girls who came in. One was Addison Thoreau, and the other was a girl he'd seen around school a lot, but he couldn't remember her name. He frowned. He sometimes worried he might be like his mom, that maybe somehow Alzheimer's was already eating away his brain and stealing his memories. He shook away that unhelpful thought and pointed out the newcomers to Seb and Booker.

"Hey, Addison!" He waved her and her friend over. "Come get a picture with us. You too, Avery!"

Avery jerked her head up from where she'd been looking at Damion's phone as if she'd been caught doing something wrong. He would've worried about her reaction except she immediately rolled her eyes at him and said, "How can I be in a picture I'm taking?"

"Did she just say that?" Seb asked. "It's almost like she doesn't know what a selfie is."

"She doesn't get out much," Damion said with a laugh.

Booker didn't laugh. He had gone perfectly still as Addison and her friend edged into the group on one side and Avery edged in on the other.

"Looks like your girlfriend isn't too busy after all," Seb whispered to Booker loudly enough that anyone paying attention would have heard.

Damion was sure Addison was paying attention. After witnessing the weird scene between Addison and Booker at lunch, he wished for Booker's sake that Seb hadn't picked that particular moment to make that particular joke.

Damion quickly draped an arm over Avery's shoulder and squeezed her into him. "If you keep calling her my girlfriend, she might give me a black eye."

Everyone whooped and catcalled at that and dared Avery to take a swing at Inside-Out Archer.

Avery stared at him with such wide-eyed surprise he thought for a moment she might really give him a black eye.

He pulled her closer and whispered in her ear, "I'll explain later."

He hated how surprised Avery looked. He would've preferred to see her blush again or maybe seem flattered or pleased. But she merely nodded and went with it.

He hoped that claiming Seb's comment about the girlfriend had worked to ease a little of Booker's evident panic.

The pictures were all finally over when Booker's mom called out, "Why don't we have Seb open his presents?"

The crowd dispersed to settle in and watch the show. Addison and her friend headed over to the food table, not that Damion could blame them, because the food was worth ignoring everyone else for.

Booker moved toward Addison, but his mom stopped him and said, "Honey, why don't you take the presents over to Seb so he has them all next to him?"

Booker nodded and obeyed.

"Poor guy," Damion whispered. He hadn't bothered moving from the fireplace. This was Seb's party and Seb's moment. He didn't want to be front and center for any of it.

"What poor guy?" Avery asked. "And what was that whole girlfriend thing?"

"Booker's bad in love with Addison Thoreau. But she's less than in love with him. At least I think so. It's hard to tell, but I figured Booker's had a hard enough day without jokes about him and Addison. And as you've kindly pointed out to me, she's had a hard enough *everything* that I don't think she needs to be teased either."

"Oh. I get it. Makes sense."

Was that disappointment in her voice? Did she maybe wish the girlfriend comment had been for some other reason? He sort of hoped so.

His day had also been hard. Not as bad as Seb's day for certain, but Damion still envied him. Seb was surrounded by friends eager to help him. How would that be? Damion had fans, not friends. Fans who didn't know what his real life was like. But being with Avery made things in his real life seem better, bearable.

"Why'd we stop being friends, Avery?"

"You got famous." She didn't look away from the crowd as she answered.

"Oh, c'mon. We stopped way before I got famous."

"I don't know, Damion. I don't remember it being any one thing. It was probably a million little things."

He considered that for a moment while they watched Seb open a gift containing a Marie Antoinette wig made out of foam. The artistry of the wig could not be denied, and Damion clapped along with the crowd. He'd never considered foam as an artistic medium before, but the wig had given him some ideas for future videos.

"It might have been a million little things that messed up our friendship. But what if it was just one thing that made us friends again?" he asked.

When she didn't answer right away, Damion glanced down to see if she'd even heard him.

She was staring up at him. "What would that one thing be?" she asked finally.

"A question—me asking you to be my friend."

Avery didn't frown, but she didn't smile either. She wrapped her arms around her middle like she had earlier when she'd been warding off the cold, even though the room with the fire and packed with so many people was far too warm.

"Why would you want that? You know what everyone says about my family, about me. Do you really want your stock to drop because of me?"

"My stock?"

"Your worth in the eyes of the masses. You think people are going to bother remembering a guy who hangs out with random nobodies?"

"You are so far from nobody, Avery. You have to know that, right?"

He edged closer and took her hand in his. He was so tired of not having anyone who knew him, really knew him. And though she didn't know the real him entirely either, she was someone he could imagine telling.

She didn't pull her hand away, which he took as a good sign. He thought about the bookmark his mom had made for him with his name on it. He'd almost lost it—would have lost it if it hadn't been for Addison.

"Anyway, it doesn't matter who remembers me and who doesn't." Those words tore at his heart as he said them. "Addison told me something this morning that has made more sense than anything else in my life. She said that it isn't about the people who remember you. It's about the people *you* remember. I remember being your friend. I'd like to try that again if you'll let me."

Another cheer went up from the crowd as a new wig emerged from a box, but neither of them looked over from their isolated spot to see what it was.

Avery made a small sound. "One thing versus a million little things, huh?"

He swallowed, worried this was her way of turning his friendship away.

"I guess it's a good thing that the one thing is big enough to eclipse all the little things, isn't it?" Avery squeezed his hand.

Just like that, Avery was his friend again. Just like that, everything was better. Everything was bearable. He wasn't alone anymore.

24

Addison's Journal
December 7, 9:02 p.m.

I'm hiding in a bathroom at Booker's house. I don't have the ability to try to guess what that means for my mental health. Is it a good sign that I'm actually facing my demons enough to *be* in Booker's house? Or is it a bad sign that my time in his house is spent hiding in his bathroom?

• •

Avery

The only thing Avery could think as she stood near the fireplace with Damion Archer's hand in hers was that Damion used to pick a flower for his mom every day on the way home from school. His mom was one of those supermoms, and she had deserved every blossom he'd tugged out of a random garden for her.

Avery hadn't meant to look, but the text came in while she was holding Damion's phone and her eyes were already on the screen. She had already been looking.

The text was from Damion's sister, Palmer. *"Dad said I owe you an apology. So I guess I'm sorry about leaving you with Mom earlier. But her Alzheimer's is hard on me in ways you can't comprehend, and I couldn't stand to see her like that for another minute today. I'll make it up to you."*

If Avery hadn't decided years earlier that Palmer was kind of the worst, that non-apology apology would have proved it.

But Damion's mom had Alzheimer's?

She couldn't stop thinking about it. She sneaked a peek at him when he busted up laughing over Seb sporting a wig that had a fleshy-looking middle and hair all around the edges, like Friar Tuck from the old *Robin Hood* movie.

Did anyone else know about Damion's mom?

She hadn't known, and she was Damion's friend. Of course, that development was pretty recent—barely ten minutes old. What had Addison told her earlier that day when Avery had insisted she wasn't Damion's friend but that maybe she would be again sometime in the future?

Next year, you'll wish you started today.

She had started their friendship today. Well, technically, *he'd* restarted their friendship. His hand in hers proved that.

He'd mentioned someone making threats and how he was worried his mom could get caught up in the mess.

She had a pretty good idea who was sending Damion hateful messages, especially after having scrolled through several of them earlier when Damion had given her permission to look at his social media messages.

Damion's messages were almost identical to the things she'd overheard some people talking about before school started. That group of people was the reason she'd decided to talk to Damion about doing his part on the Hope Squad. Rhett Morgan had been the biggest talker of the group. He'd sounded pretty hateful and completely unhinged. He was the sort of guy to make threats and worse. If she was right about the messages being from that guy, what could she do about it?

She excused herself by saying she needed to use the restroom, but when she tried the door handle, it was locked.

Avery wanted to slink away because she hated having to face the person in the bathroom whenever they came out. She knew it was an absurd thing to worry about, but she always felt like the person who'd been rushed in the restroom would secretly loathe her for jiggling the door and cutting their time short.

Not that any of her thoughts were grounded in reality. She didn't hate the people who jiggled the handle when she was in a restroom, so why would they despise her? Sense or not, she hated it and was about to turn and come back later when the door swung open and Addison Thoreau walked out.

"Sorry," Addison said. "I just . . ."

They stared awkwardly at one another for a moment. Avery wanted to tell Addison about Damion, about how they'd made up and were having some weird sort of do-over on their friendship. She wanted to thank Addison but had no idea how to explain anything, so she smiled instead.

Addison bobbed her head in response and moved down the hall.

Avery stepped into the bathroom and locked the door. "I am so wicked absurd. I really gotta learn how to talk to people," she said out loud.

She lowered the toilet lid and sat, unlocked her phone, found the contact she still had from when she'd tutored Rhett Morgan in algebra, and typed out a text.

"Hey, I heard you're threatening Damion Archer."

The immediate response surprised her. *"Who this?"*

Seriously? She was the whole reason this jackbag was going to graduate because there was no way he'd have passed that class without her. And he couldn't have bothered to save her number in his phone?

Not that she really blamed him. She was too lazy to delete contacts, which was why she still had his number.

"I'm Addison Thoreau's friend. And when Damion told her what you were doing, she said she was going to talk to the principal. She's super furious."

It was technically a lie. Not even technically. Everything she'd written was a blatant lie. All of it. Avery couldn't even claim to be Addison's friend. Not really. Though she felt friendship toward Addison, they were skimming the surface of acquaintance. Avery would have to remedy that. Not only because she felt Addison needed friends but also because the day had taught her how much *she* needed them as well.

"I care she's furious?" There had been a delay in his response, which Avery took to mean that Rhett was considering how legit her texts might be.

"You'll care when you're suspended for cyberbullying. Did you know threatening someone with bodily injury is a criminal offense? You could go to jail for that. You'll definitely care when your dad finds out and cuts you off because you're such a disappointment."

It was a low blow to include Rhett's father, a district attorney who would not like his son to embarrass him, but Rhett had started it, and if anything would shut the guy down, it was the fear of his father.

"It's not like Archer has proof."

Avery smiled. Those were the words of the guilty. *"Except he does. You should have been smarter when sending those messages.*

They link right back to you. You clearly have no clue what you're doing."

Rhett took several more minutes to respond, only to offer a vulgar suggestion of what she could do with her information.

She turned her phone off, feeling pretty good about how it had gone down. The vulgarity was Rhett's brain-dead way of saving face. But she felt certain the texts and messages sent to Damion would now be at an end.

She exited the bathroom and made her way back to Damion. He was laughing at something, his head thrown back. When she stood next to him again and he looked down at her, she swallowed. When had Damion grown so tall?

They stayed on the sidelines as the final gifts were opened. Avery felt surprised when the last present was announced as having come from Addison. Addison seemed as much on the sidelines of the party as Avery and Damion. Booker looked as surprised as Avery felt.

The wig she'd brought was a spikey thing made out of blue cardboard. It looked like something Jack Frost would wear.

Damion leaned over to whisper, "Clever artwork."

She agreed.

Seb loved it, and Booker . . . well, Avery thought he did too, but his expression was unreadable.

"It's time, boys," Seb shouted, gesturing for his friends to take their seats next to him. The hum of clippers filled the room.

A cry of dismay erupted from the crowd when the first clumps of hair fell to the ground, but Seb was grinning. A hushed silence fell over the room until there was nothing except the buzz of clippers.

"C'mon, everyone," Seb said. "It's okay to come right out

and say it. No reason to worry about hurting anyone's feelings here. I have the best-looking bald head here."

Everyone laughed, and the moment of painful reverence lifted.

"Time to go?" she asked Damion when it was all over. She loved that the party atmosphere remained even with the heads shaved.

"I think we've adequately shown our support," he whispered back. He caught Booker's eye and gestured to the door. Booker nodded a quick acknowledgment that it was okay they were leaving. Damion led her to the front door. No one noticed them gather their coats and sneak out.

"You okay?" he asked, likely because she was so quiet.

It almost made her cry to hear Damion ask such a question considering all he had going on in his own life. She had so misjudged him. They crunched over the frozen ground as they walked toward his car; they'd been forced to park at the end of the street because of all the people who'd come to the party.

"I need to confess something," she said.

"Can you promise it's something truly humiliating for you because, otherwise, I don't want to hear it." He tossed her a sideways smile.

She didn't have the heart to banter with him. "I read a message on your phone from Palmer. It was about your mom. I didn't mean to read it, but I was already looking at your phone when it came in, and I'm literate, so it's not like I can't *not* read words when I see them. It just happens. Anyway, I wanted you to know I knew because I hate lying, and I suck at keeping secrets from people, and you said you wanted to be friends, which means being honest with each other—at least it does to me—so I know you're hurting, and I want to know how to help or what to say, or maybe ask permission to beat up Palmer for being a jackbag about your pain."

He kept walking. He didn't slow or stop like she thought he might when he heard she knew.

"Damion?"

He didn't answer, just kept walking until he made it to his car. "How do you see a text and just know?" he asked quietly. "Palmer doesn't know. She sends me messages like that all the time, talking about how hard Mom's Alzheimer's is on her. She doesn't get it. She doesn't have a clue what it's doing to me." He leaned against the car. "She doesn't remember me—my mom. She doesn't remember my name. Palmer doesn't know what that does to me."

Avery had never seen Damion so unraveled. She'd been through plenty of emotions with him when they were kids, but she didn't know how to handle this version of him.

He stood before her, his breath coming out in sharp, frozen puffs.

She thought of the bookmark Addison had picked up off the floor earlier that day. He'd been so visibly shaken by the idea of losing a bookmark with his name on it. Chances were good his mom made it for him or had given it to him. And what had Avery done? She'd privately made fun of him for having a big ego. She'd had it all wrong. It wasn't ego. It was fear.

"That's why," she said softly as she took his hand.

"Why what?"

"The fame thing. The need to be the center of everyone's universe. The selfies. The constant updates. Your need for social media acceptance stems from wanting to matter somewhere, to make a mark on the world so big that people can't forget you."

"No. Not entirely. People expect me to be like this. I have

to have a social media presence or I end up losing my audience, and then I'm out of a job." He paused, then said quietly, "I pay for a lot of her medical bills."

He didn't pull his hand away. She half expected him to since she'd basically accused him of being the same sort of faker that Rhett had accused him of being.

He took a deep breath and released it in a long line of steam. "But you're not entirely wrong. I *am* afraid of being forgotten. I'm sorry. I didn't mean to freak out. I haven't had to talk to anyone about this before. I'm handling it badly."

"I'm your friend, Archer, not your fan. And not saying I'm super good at knowing how friendship works since I don't have any friends other than you, but I think it's okay to handle it badly if you need to. I'm sorry about your mom. She was always so nice to me. She never treated me like I was from the wrong neighborhood. And when my mom died, she always invited me to stay for dinner as if she knew I was pretty much fending for myself because my dad worked so much." She grinned. "And she didn't think I was a delinquent when I borrowed your go-kart."

"*Stole* my go-kart."

Avery tugged his hand as she nodded to the car. "We should really discuss this where we have access to a heater."

Once they were in his car and the heater was running, she asked, "Will you do me a favor?"

"That seems to be the question of the day from you."

She laughed. "I left my motorcycle at school. I need to get it. Would you give me a ride?"

"No."

She was about to get mad at him when he added, "It's late and cold. I'll pick you up in the morning and take you to school."

She agreed and let the silence settle between them because she didn't know what to say. He drummed his fingers on the steering wheel as he drove, his lips pressed together. It was unfair that she knew so much more about him than she had this morning when she had not given him the same chance to know her.

"You won't get any more messages from the person who's been giving you a rough time today."

His eyes left the road to look at her in surprise. "How do you know?"

"I texted him and told him you were going to press charges if even one more thing showed up."

"How did you know who—?"

"I heard some guys talking about you this morning before school. That was how I knew to warn you that people were spreading rumors. I figured it was the one doing most of the talking, and I was right."

He flipped on his blinker. "Just like when we were little. You have always been good at standing up to bullies. I'm sorry I was a jerk when you gave me the heads-up this morning. I shouldn't have said the things I did."

Avery shrugged. "You just said what everyone thinks. Everybody expects you to be the selfie-taking rock star. Everybody expects me to be the delinquent on her way to jail. People expect me to be like my brother. And while, yes, my brother's made some seriously stupid choices, he's not everything they think he is either."

"It's gotta be tough—dealing with people expecting the worst from you all the time."

"Not everyone does. I have some teachers who think I've got good things ahead of me."

He glanced at her again. "I think I agree with them."

"Do you?" She hated how desperate for affirmation she sounded, but she couldn't deny that it felt good to hear it.

"I really do. Who else would put up with me being a jerk, take in a homeless mother and baby, and then resolve my cyberbullying for me all in one day?"

"I *am* pretty amazing," Avery said. "But not always. I don't know why my brother going to jail made me reach the inner circles of Irrational Town, but it really did."

"Family can do that to you."

They pulled up in front of Avery's house. She wasn't ashamed of it like she had been when he'd come to pick her up. That was the thing about being friends again. She knew he wasn't judging her.

Which was why she had the courage to ask, "Will you come with me when I visit my brother this weekend? I'd hoped I'd have news about maybe getting him out on bail, but I think he'll be just as glad to hear Dad and I are taking care of Jo and the baby. I mean, I'm pretty sure Jo and the baby will come, too, but I'd like you there anyway."

"Sure. And maybe later you can come to dinner at my house and help me entertain my mom."

"I'm in. I already told you I love your mom."

"She won't remember you."

Avery had her hand on the door handle. "What was it Addison told you? It's about the people you remember, not the other way around?"

Damion nodded. She opened the car door and was surprised when he opened his as well. He walked her to the front porch, falling into step next to her. She liked that he walked beside her. She liked that she wasn't walking alone. She liked that inside her house, her family was bigger. She liked that she would see her brother that weekend while being surrounded by friends and love and people who would help her help him.

She planned on sending Damion another text before she went to bed, thanking him for everything.

She liked knowing he would text her back.

25

Addison's Journal
December 7, 9:29 p.m.

I'm in the bathroom again. I have no excuses.

Seeing Booker with his mom makes me think about my mom. My therapist brings up my mom all the time. It's like she wants me to say there's something wrong with that relationship, but—

No. That's not true. She knows my mom loves me. It's obvious. It's obvious to everyone.

And everyone knows I love my mom. It's not like I wanted to leave her, exactly. I just wanted to give her the chance to live her life. About a month before I did what I did, a guy who works at the hardware store—I think he owns the store, actually—anyway, he asked my mom out on a date.

It's not the first time that's happened. My mom is really pretty. She looks good for a woman her age. I mean really good. People always say we could be sisters. And they're totally right. But my mom doesn't date. Not ever. Like, not ever ever.

And I know why. It's not like I don't get it. I totally do. I just wish . . . it was different. I wish there were parts of our lives where we were really normal. But the lack of romantic love in my mom's life is proof that we are not normal. It's proof that she never got over things either. She's afraid of letting anyone in because she's afraid they will hurt me. So we're stuck in this weird place.

The hardware guy who asked her out? He's a really nice guy. You can tell. People give off creepy vibes when they're creepy and nice vibes when they're nice. At least I think they do. Because it kind of feels that way for me. Intuition, maybe?

Hazel told me once that intuition is just your brain processing faster than you can consciously keep up and so you should trust yourself when it comes to how you feel about people.

Hardware Guy is nice. And my mom should have said yes. But she looked over at me. It's not like I saw her look at me because I was pretending to be really, really interested in a display of Estwing hammers—and totally eavesdropping.

But I felt it when my mom's gaze fell on me. It was like a heavy blanket on a too-hot day. It was a suffocating weight. And I heard her say she was busy. I heard her thank him for the compliment, but she really wasn't interested in pursuing relationships of that nature at this time.

And it killed me a little bit.

Long before I did what I did, I was already dying.

As much as I want a real relationship with a good guy for my mom, I want it for myself too. Booker haunts my every step, my every thought. Reminding me that I cannot have that relationship.

But I still want it.

A lot.

Booker is a good guy. My intuition, or my brain processing faster than I can process, tells me what I want to know about him. Yes, someone hurt me. But that someone wasn't Booker. Maybe it's time to trust him. Maybe it's time to trust me and how I feel about him. Maybe if I can figure out my life, my mom will be able to get her own, and no one will have to die.

Some people are determined to do everything—the FOMO people. They're busy trying to shove everything in, but they never seem to really enjoy it, like a dog eating a steak, gulping it down without tasting it. I think I'm the opposite. I think I take too long to chew each bite, and the steak is now cold, and I'm not enjoying it either.

There's got to be something in the middle.

I'm in the ocean, the current tugging me under, and I'm drowning *and* waving at the people on the shore. But aren't we all like that? Is anyone actually on the shore? Or are we all drowning and waving and hoping someone will see us? Rescue us?

And even if someone did want to rescue me, haven't I been out in the ocean much too far for most of my life? Much too far to rescue?

No one heard her—the dead girl.

I'm not waving, but I'm not drowning anymore either.

It's time to learn how to swim.

· ·

Addison Thoreau

Addison unlocked the bathroom door and peered into the hallway. No one was waiting, which was good. She'd been in there a long time. It would have been embarrassing to have to face them.

She joined the others in the living room. Hazel was laughing with some of Seb's friends from his school. Addison didn't want to interrupt her when she was obviously having a good time.

She looked around for Damion and that other girl—Avery, who had been waiting outside the bathroom before—but they must have left. She bit back her disappointment. It would have been good to have people she knew-ish to talk to. She would have to look for her at school and find a reason to have a real conversation where she wasn't sputtering cryptic gratitude.

231

"Thanks for coming."

Booker's voice from behind her startled her, but she didn't jump. She turned slowly. She wasn't sure if her careful movements were to keep him from running off or to keep *her* from running off. He'd been standing off to the side of the Christmas tree, hidden by branches loaded with ornaments. Booker's mom was one of those designer moms—the kind where everything in her house matched and made sense.

Once she was facing Booker, she wasn't sure what to say. She glanced at his smooth, bald head, then quickly looked away. He looked nice with no hair. Addison noticed a thin ridge on his scalp just above his left ear—a scar his hair had hidden. She wondered if he wanted to stare at her wrists the same way she wanted to stare at his head.

"I'm glad I came. Your cousin seems nice."

"He is nice." Booker glanced over at Seb. A shadow passed over Booker's expression. It didn't go away when he turned his attention back to her. "I didn't think you were going to be here."

"Why? Because you don't think I have the ability to care about anyone else maybe dying?" She didn't know why she was turning the conversation into an argument. She didn't know why she felt so much sudden rage.

Booker inhaled sharply and glanced back to where everyone was still rubbing Seb's bald head as if he might start granting wishes. When it seemed no one had heard her, he lowered his voice. "Of course not."

She wished she knew how to talk without being a mess. "I'm sorry. Look, Booker, I didn't come here to fight with you. I came to . . . I don't know. I just wanted to explain what happened and let you know it isn't your fault. I've had some crappy things happen to me in the past, and it's going to take some time for me to sort it all out. Anyway, I don't think we should hang out until I get stuff figured out if that's okay with you."

She didn't know why she'd said all that. She'd had no intention of saying any of that. She had meant to come over and make up with Booker in a way that allowed them to still be friends. But because her temper was out of control for stupid reasons, she was doing it all wrong.

"It's not okay with me."

She was as surprised by the words as by the soft, gentle delivery of them. After her outburst, it would have been fair for him to retaliate with an argument. She supposed he kind of *was* arguing, declaring it wasn't okay with him to not spend time together.

"It's not that I don't get it, Addison," he said. "Because I do. Get it, I mean. You've had crappy things happen, and you want to work through them. I want to help you with that."

"What makes you think you can?" Why? Why did she sound so angry even to her own ears?

He reached up and absently twirled an ornament, making it glitter with the reflection of the tree lights. "Sometimes at the shelter, we get dogs who've had bad things happen to them. Dogs who don't trust anyone. They don't stop being afraid when we leave them alone. They only get more afraid. They only stop being afraid when we spend time with them, when we help them work through it. I want you to be happy. I don't think being alone is going to help you work through anything."

She wished they weren't in his living room, surrounded by his family and friends. It prevented her from raising her voice like she wanted. "I'm not a dog, Booker. What I've been through isn't even close to the same thing."

"I would never say it was. But the nice thing about being

human is that you can have other humans help—humans who care about you."

"Humans like you?"

He stopped fiddling with the ornament and met her eyes. "Yeah. Like me."

His words didn't make her less mad, though she was sure he'd expected them to.

"How can you help me? Look at you, Book; you can't even help yourself. You keep looking at Seb with big, mopey eyes like he's going to fall down dead in the next thirty seconds. He doesn't need that from you. He doesn't need the burden of being strong for everyone else. You have your whole life to break down about him possibly dying. How are *you* supposed to help *me*?"

She shouldn't have said it. Why was she angry? Why was she angry with him? None of this was Booker's fault. He didn't deserve to be called out for no good reason. How could she call her words back? How could she fix what she'd said? The Christmas music in the background seemed to mock her, and the lights and beauty of the room felt too bright, too perfect, too suffocating.

"You're right," Booker's soft response made her feel worse. "I'm not handling the thought of losing him very well. I'm not handling the thought of losing you very well either. I just want you to know you're not alone. And if you say that space away from me is what you need, then okay. But even then you're still not alone. Because I'm here whenever you need me."

He shifted, and Addison thought he might reach out again, might try to touch her in some way, but he didn't.

"I'm sorry if everything I've said sucks as bad as I think it does, but I don't really know how to explain what I feel about you."

She didn't know why his words felt like he'd held out his

hand and offered to take some of the fire from her burning secrets. "What *do* you feel about me? What does it matter to you
if I live or die?"

She felt like a balloon, her string unwinding from the hand
tethering it to the earth. What if he let go of the string altogether and she floated away? She wouldn't blame him if he did
let go after she'd snapped at him.

Booker tilted his head and looked at her just like he had a
few months back when she'd felt seen by him for the first time.
"You ever hear the song 'One More Light' by Linkin Park?"

She shook her head.

"It basically asks who cares if one more light goes out in
a sky of a million stars. Because if there are a million stars out
there, what difference does one make? But I care. One light
makes all the difference. Ever since the day you moved into
town and walked into Colby's science class, I've wanted to know
you, to talk to you, to hear you say my name. I feel *everything*
about you."

She'd never seen Booker get emotional. She'd never seen his
eyes tear up the way they did now.

He let out a breath that seemed like he'd been holding it forever. "Addison, I want to be there for you, but in order for me to
do that, I need you to be here. I need you to stay. I'm not saying
you won't have more bad stuff in your future. I can't promise
that, but I can promise that there will be good things too. I just
don't want to see you miss the good."

She didn't respond. She didn't know how. What she did
know was that her anger was gone. She'd held that anger for so
long without even realizing it that she wasn't sure what to do
without it sitting in her chest, fueling her fires.

He rushed on as if needing to fill her silence. "It's not like

I need anything else *except* to be your friend. To talk to you, to ruin lunches for teachers with you, to study and skip classes and just be friends," he said. "You tell me what you need, and I will help you get it."

She nodded, thinking of what all that meant. "Thank you." The two words rasped in her throat, feeling like they got caught on something as they tried to escape.

He gave a small shake of his head, confused. His eyebrows pinched together, looking strange compared to the baldness of his head.

She tried to explain. "Thank you for seeing me wave."

If he'd looked confused before, that statement didn't clear anything up for him.

"I've spent a lot of years of people telling me what I need. I'm not used to anyone actually listening when I have an opinion on the subject. I'm sorry I snapped a minute ago. None of what's wrong with me is your fault." Addison's gaze slipped to where Seb was getting more pictures. "And none of what's wrong with him is your fault either."

Booker let out a strangled chuckle. "I know that."

She kept her voice gentle, matching Booker's soft tone. "I hope you do. Because, Booker? I think I can speak for Seb in this after having watched you do everything in your power to make him feel comfortable and knowing all you've done today to make *me* feel comfortable—we're lucky to have you on our side."

Addison didn't realize the truth of her words until she said them out loud. She was lucky to have Booker on her side.

Hazel looked up from her conversation and caught Addison's eye. She flicked a glance from Addison to Booker and back. She raised her eyebrows in question, and Addison nodded to let Hazel know she was ready to go.

Addison blew out a long breath. "I need to let you get back to your party and pay attention to the guest of honor."

His entire demeanor deflated, which would have been cute if she hadn't become hyperaware of people and emotions and waving and drowning.

"But I'll see you tomorrow." She hesitated before adding, "I'll *talk* to you tomorrow. And this is going to sound weird, but is it okay if I touch your head?"

He barked out a nervous laugh and lowered his head. She placed her fingers against his smooth scalp and lightly brushed them over his dark skin, tracing the scar-like ridge. "I'm sorry we didn't talk before you shaved your hair all off. I really wanted to tug on your curls like you do when you're reading."

"There's always later. It'll grow back."

She lowered her hand. "Yes. There's always later."

Hazel joined them, thanked Booker for the great party, and gave Booker a hug.

Addison didn't hug him, but she felt like they'd come to an understanding, a good place. Cracked and broken yet still whole, she thought maybe she and Booker had a chance at real friendship.

When she got home, her mom was in the living room, sitting in the chair by the Christmas tree. The branches held ornaments that were tattered and scattered—a lot like everything else in their lives. It was not at all like the designer tree at Booker's house, but it was exactly like the tree she felt belonged in theirs.

Her mom looked up, her eyes tired and red. She'd likely been crying while Addison was away.

"Oh, hey. You're home," her mother said, her voice thick,

her nose sounding stuffy. She had definitely been crying. "How was it?"

"Good." Addison opened her mouth to say more but found herself swallowing her words back down.

"Good. I found a bottle of glue that hadn't already dried up, but not until after you left. It would have been useful for your art project, but hopefully it'll stay fresh for the next one."

Addison nodded and tried again to say the words she'd only thought about saying to her mom—the words her therapist encouraged her to say out loud. All that came out of her mouth was a hiss of air.

She tried again. "Mom?"

The whispered word felt like glass shards scratching up her throat.

Her mom smoothed her hands over the romance novel on her lap. "Hmm?"

Was it too hot in the living room? She usually thought it was too cold because they saved money by not keeping the heat up too high. But at the moment, it was so, so hot. "I want to talk about . . . it."

Her mom's hands stilled, then she curled her fingers around her book. "About . . . going to the hospital?" Her mom always referred to her attempt that way.

"Well that too. But I'm ready to talk about *it*. About him. About what he did to me and why we left."

Her mom's eyes widened, and Addison felt certain that if her mother hadn't been sitting, she would have stumbled back and knocked over the Christmas tree. There was fear in her mother's eyes. Addison hurried to ease that fear into something else.

"It isn't your fault. What he did wasn't your fault. And it wasn't my fault."

That was how she started the conversation they had needed to have for years.

They talked for a long time. Addison worried she had kept her mom up late, considering she had to work in the morning, but her mom hugged her and assured her that she would sleep better than she had in a long time.

Addison was sure *she* would sleep better too.

When she finally went to her room for the night, she turned off her light and opened her blinds so she could see the sky. Even with the light pollution from the city, there were a lot of stars. What was it Booker had said? That her one light in a sky of a million stars mattered?

But there weren't just a million stars in the human family. There were more than eight billion. In a sky of a billion stars—in eight billion stars—did she still matter?

She felt certain Booker would say the answer was yes.

When it came to all the other stars out there, she would say yes as well.

But how did she feel about her own light?

. . . .

Addison's Journal
December 8, 12:02 a.m.

What a day. The journal thing helped me get through it. At least I think it did. It's not like the journal showed anything special about me the way that the therapist said it would. But it helped me sort through my feelings.

The day was weirdly ordinary as far as days go. I mean, nothing spectacular happened, but I feel better. Sometimes a little thing like feeling better actually feels spectacular because it means I'm still here. And it's dumb that I feel like I have all sorts of reasons to celebrate because it's not like me staying alive helps anyone.

Not true.

It helps my mom. I now know that much is true. I think talking about the hard things will be good for us. It'll be awhile before we're good at that if tonight was any indicator, but it's a start.

I felt like talking to her helped her as much as it helped me. And maybe in the future, I will have the ability to find a way to help others as much as people helped me today. Maybe?

I'm pretty sure Carl Sagan's quote about how everyone is made of star-stuff wasn't just so people could hang a pretty platitude on their wall. Everyone is fundamentally the same, made from the dust of long-dead stars. And maybe we shine just as brightly. Maybe, if we let ourselves, we can shine even brighter.

I'm in a good place. A place where I'm not drowning. A place where I'm not swimming either. Not yet. But I am treading water today.

No one heard her, the dead girl.

But I'm not dead.

I'm still here.

And I'm staying.

Author's Note

Suicide is a painful and serious public concern that can have long-lasting consequences for individuals, families, and communities. It is devastating to all involved. The good news is that suicide is preventable if people from all walks of life and places within society are paying attention and striving to be a part of the solution.

According to the CDC, everyone can be a part of the solution and help prevent suicide by learning the warning signs, promoting prevention and resilience, and committing to social change.

If you or someone you know is thinking about suicide or needs help, call or text toll-free the Suicide and Crisis Lifeline: 988.

It's free and confidential. You'll be connected to a skilled, trained counselor in your area. You are not alone. Talk to someone now. Remember, it's just three numbers: 9-8-8.

You are important to this world. You have a light that only *you* can give.

Stay and shine!

Acknowledgments

This book has been a long time in the works for me and has taken several pivots and restarts before I felt confident enough to turn it in to my publisher.

Mental health is a tricky subject. How personal do I want to get with my own struggles? How do I keep this story fictitious while also being true? I hope the end result is something that provides a candle flame of hope to those who feel lost in the darkness of their own minds and circumstances.

I want to thank those early readers who helped me mold this book into its current shape: Crystal Liechty, Heather Moore, Gary Peterson, Sara Crowe, Josi Kilpack, Jeff and Jen Savage, James Dashner, and my own three children: Mckenna, Merrik, and Chandler. And to my daughter-in-law Charisma and the many other sensitivity readers who gave valuable insight on writing a diverse cast. You all were immensely helpful with feedback and support. Thank you.

It was humbling to receive feedback from my publisher on this particular book. To have them so resoundingly excited about this project filled me with gratitude for the amazing people they are. Thank you, Heidi Taylor, Chris Schoebinger, Lisa Mangum, Dennis Gaunt, Troy Butcher, Callie Hansen, and the rest of the

ACKNOWLEDGMENTS

Shadow Mountain family for your vision, guidance, and genuine desire to bring light into the world.

Also, I can never be grateful enough to the most important stars in my personal sky: Scott, McKenna, Dwight, Merrik, Charisma, Chandler, Julianna, Theo, Lily, and Mom and Dad. You all support me as a writer and as a human, and you don't mind when I have "Eeyore" and "bad MS" days. I love you all so much.

And last, but never least, thank you, Heavenly Father, for being aware of me in my darkest hour of depression, for stepping in and saving my life, and for being aware of us all and loving us all.

Discussion Questions

1. Everyone believes Damion has the perfect life, but they don't see the struggles he goes through. Other people believe Avery will never amount to much. In what ways do we judge those around us for good or bad? How can we leave behind our judgments and really get to know people?

2. Because Addison has bottled up her pain for as long as she can remember, it is difficult for her to make meaningful connections. How can we be open and honest in our relationships with others without sharing too much too soon?

3. All of the characters are going through something difficult in their private lives. Through Addison, they are able to rise above their struggles and find connections, but Addison never truly understands how she improved the lives of those around her just by existing for that one day. Has there ever been a time when someone did something extraordinary for you, though the act seemed small and inconsequential to the giver?

4. There are several characters in this book who feel isolated and unseen. What are some ways we can strive to be inclusive and "see" people?

5. Addison struggles with feeling her own worth, and she

worries she doesn't have anything to offer, though the reader can see how incredibly important she is. What are some ways we can alter our own self-talk so we can feel our worth?

6. Addison is finally able to help herself when she realizes she isn't waving to people on the shore while she is in the middle of the ocean but, rather, she is drowning. She learns that everyone is trying to keep from drowning in their own oceans and everyone needs help. How can we gain empathy and compassion for others, and how can we share that empathy and compassion?

7. In the classic film *It's a Wonderful Life*, George Bailey discovers what the world would be like if he had never been born. In what ways does *Swimming in a Sea of Stars* parallel Addison with George Bailey? In what ways would the lives of the other characters be diminished if Addison had not survived her attempt?

8. Addison comes to understanding the importance of each individual star in the sky, which changes how she sees herself and her life. What are some ways you might also embrace your importance as a valuable individual?